The Art of Being Broken

by

Nicole Sorrell

The Art of Living, Book Two

Copyright Notice
This is a work of fiction. Names, characters, places, and incidents are either the product of the author's imagination or are used fictitiously, and any resemblance to actual persons living or dead, business establishments, events, or locales, is entirely coincidental.

The Art of Being Broken

COPYRIGHT © 2024 by Nicole Sorrell

All rights reserved. No part of this book may be used or reproduced in any manner whatsoever without written permission of the author or The Wild Rose Press, Inc. except in the case of brief quotations embodied in critical articles or reviews.
Contact Information: info@thewildrosepress.com

Cover Art by *The Wild Rose Press, Inc.*

The Wild Rose Press, Inc.
PO Box 708
Adams Basin, NY 14410-0708
Visit us at www.thewildrosepress.com

Publishing History
First Edition, 2024
Trade Paperback ISBN 978-1-5092-5804-8
Digital ISBN 978-1-5092-5805-5

The Art of Living, Book Two
Published in the United States of America

Prologue

Monday, July 20
"...Why didn't you just tell me what had happened?" I ask Angeline.

On the deck of Father's house, we sit on the steps leading down to the back yard.

"I thought it would be better if you found out little by little," she says. "If I told you all at once...Well, would you have believed it?"

"I would've believed you." I bite my lip. "But you're right, it would've been a lot to absorb in one sitting." After a moment, I add, "I'll never be able to forgive them."

"You will, Maddie. It'll take a while. You have to, though. Promise?"

"I can't promise that. How is it possible to pardon that kind of evil?" Angeline has such a sad expression that I relent. "Okay. For you, I'll try." I don't tell her I'd vowed to make Father pay for what he'd done.

She nods, accepting my compromise. We listen for a time to the hypnotic rhythm of cicada calls. Crickets saw, and occasionally a frog croons, adding to the song of the new-washed country night. I gaze up at the partly cloudy sky. I can't put off my question any longer.

"Does this mean you won't talk to me anymore?" Part of me doesn't want to let her go, despite the implications for my sanity.

"Do you want me to?"

My chin quivers and tears spill. How can I say goodbye? I didn't realize how final it would be. I'll never be comforted by her again or hear her contagious giggle. Never see her eyes dance when she smiles. I say nothing.

"I know," she whispers. "I'll miss you, too."

Pulling her into a hug, I rest my cheek on her hair. "I love you, Angeline."

"Love you more, Maddie..."

Chapter One

Friday, September 18
I didn't want to be here.

My mouth went dry as I knocked at Bobby Wittford's front door and waited. When he saw me, I hoped his response wouldn't be violent.

Instead of Bobby, a woman answered. In her early forties, her leathery skin was too weather-beaten to be pretty. Her hair was a mousy brown, and her voice sounded like a smoker's.

"We don't need what you're selling." She started to shut the door.

"I'm a friend of Bobby's," I blurted. *So much for your promise of honesty.* "Is he home?"

She gave me an appraising look. "You Stephany?"

"No. I'm Madisen." Remembering how Bobby's six-year-old son, Tony, had greeted me, I stuck out my hand. "Very pleased to meet you."

Shaking it, she relaxed. "Hi. I'm Amber. Bobby's not home right now. He ran to the store."

A little blond boy pushed his way around Amber. "Hi!" he said.

"Hi, there. Nice to see you again, Tony. I don't know if you remember me."

" 'Course, I remember," Tony replied, as if I'd insulted his intelligence. "You're Madisen." Amber's lips arced up when Tony admitted he knew me. It took years off her.

"Do you expect Bobby home soon?"

"He should be back any minute. Come on in and have a seat."

Sitting by Tony on the frayed sofa, I had second thoughts about my decision to see Bobby. It had certainly caused trouble with my boyfriend, Zac, and had led to our first big fight. *Maybe you should've listened to him.*

I'd just arrived in Missouri, and we'd argued during the two-hour drive to Clantonville from the Kansas City airport. I asked to borrow Zac's truck. If I didn't confront Bobby before the bachelorette party that night, apprehension would spoil my fun.

"Where do you need to go?" Zac asked, curiosity reflecting in his chocolate eyes.

I gritted my teeth, afraid the subject might cause a disagreement. Prompted by my therapist, I'd adopted a new personal rule to be honest about my feelings, especially with people I was close to. My visit with Zac would put it to the test.

"I'm going to Winnser. I need to talk to Bobby Wittford." Two months ago, I'd reported Bobby to the police, certain he was the vandal who damaged the house I'd just inherited. However, I'd also been convinced his father had murdered my sister Angeline. I'd been wrong about her killer's identity, which led me to believe I'd misjudged Bobby as well. I felt I owed him an apology.

I was mistaken about Zac's reaction. It went far beyond a difference of opinion. The defined muscles in his arms bunched as he launched into overprotective, testosterone-driven, macho man.

"The hell you are, Maddie!" he shouted. "I'm not letting you get close to that son of a bitch. Didn't you learn your lesson? He threatened you. Almost pushed you backward down the porch steps."

"Don't tell me what to do!" I yelled back.

"Don't take risks that could get you hurt. Your judgment is way out of line on this."

I flinched at the cutting remark. I didn't know whether to cry because Zac thought so little of me or get mad at myself for being too sensitive.

The anger won, though my trembling voice revealed I was close to tears. That irritated me even more. In the last ten weeks, I'd cried more than the previous twenty-eight years of my life.

"Don't insult my decisions," I said. "If you insist on being cruel, I won't tell you my plans. I'll ask to borrow Tabitha's car."

Guilt etched his face. "I'm sorry. That was thoughtless of me."

To let him know he wasn't off the hook, I responded by crossing my arms.

He added, "I'm afraid you'll get hurt. No way I can let that happen. You know it would tear me apart."

"Your words bruised me more than Bobby Wittford ever could. And he's not someone who claims to care about me."

"God. You're right, I apologize." He rubbed his jaw, trying to erase his frustration. "You may not think you need to be kept safe. But what happened during your last visit brings out my protective instincts."

His point was valid. During my last visit, I'd spent a week in the hospital with a bullet wound. I'd just discovered Father had been molesting my sister before she died. I'd screamed threats, promising to send him to prison as a pedophile. If that weren't possible, I'd ruin his law practice by getting him disbarred. In hindsight, a little restraint might've prevented me getting shot. *Oh well. Add subtlety to the list of things you need to work on.*

"That doesn't mean you can tell me what to do." I pulled my hair behind my shoulders. "And you won't need to protect me. I'm going to apologize to Bobby for causing him trouble in July."

"He doesn't deserve it." Zac's knuckles turned white on the steering wheel. "When Dad finds out you've talked to Wittford, I won't be able to defuse his temper like last time. He'll be furious."

"He won't find out unless you tell him. You're not going to change my mind. We might as well drop it."

"Fine," he said, staring ahead. "I'll go with you."

"Oh, no, you won't. Don't make me call you a 'sasshole.' " I tried to derail the argument with our personal humor. "Besides, stubbornness is one of my best qualities," I teased. The mood had lightened somewhat, though he still looked concerned.

"You are stubborn, I'll grant you that. If I go with you, I can make sure you won't be harmed." Instinctively starting to object, I clamped down on the gut reaction. He was compromising. The least I could do was meet him halfway.

"Okay. How about you drop me off at his house? If you agree not to sit in the truck outside, I promise I'll call if Bobby doesn't behave like a gentleman."

He didn't reply for a long time, finally grumbling, "Fine."

"Thank you. However, you need to show how

much you regret criticizing me."

"Can you forgive me?" He glanced at me to gauge my mood. "When your safety is on the line, I go a little crazy. How can I make it up to you?"

I raised a brow suggestively. "You'll have to get on your knees and grovel when we get to your place."

"I'll do more than grovel when I'm on my knees." Raw desire radiated from him as he brushed a finger over my thigh. "Baby, I'll apologize over and over and over."

When we'd arrived at Zac's house, he'd done just that.

Amber broke into my reflections, handing me a glass of iced tea. I thanked her, hearing the sound of a car outside. Guessing it was Bobby, I was relieved. At last, I could get this over with.

I should've known better.

Bobby came in the back door. His footfalls paused, and the refrigerator door opened and closed. When his heavy tread came into the living room, he seemed to take up the whole space. I'd forgotten what a tall, muscular man he was. At six feet four, he was ten inches taller than me. He saw me sitting next to Tony.

"What the...What are you doing here?" He stalked toward me, hands fisted.

"I came to apologize," I said, hoping to curb his anger. He stopped short with an open mouth. "Can we talk?" I nodded toward Tony to indicate we should speak in private.

Bobby's confusion was clear as he opened the door for me onto the front porch. An evening breeze had smoothed the jagged heat. It would be a pleasant evening. There were no chairs. I sat on the narrow concrete steps. From there, it would be easier to get away if he tried to hit me.

Bobby settled beside me. His broad shoulder nudged mine, raising my anxiety another notch. The sleeves of his T-shirt rode up, abandoning their effort to stretch over his biceps. Sitting close, I admired the color of his eyes. Gold with a little green, they were fascinating and mysterious. I was sure he got a lot of female attention. He'd certainly seized mine, despite my nerves.

I let him start the conversation. He demanded, "What the hell are you doing here?"

"As I said, I wanted to apologize for telling the police I thought you'd trashed my house in Clantonville. The words 'leave,' 'get out,' and 'go away' were painted on the walls. You said bringing up Angeline's murder would cause problems, and you could lose Tony. It made sense you were the one trying to drive me out."

Bobby's eyes saucered as if he hadn't considered this. Then he squinted at his boots like he wanted to burn holes in them. Voice low, he said, "I was pissed at you when the police showed up. They left it alone when the owner of the pool hall backed me up, saying I spent the night there on the couch. It didn't start a hassle with Tony's mom." He started to fidget. "I guess I should also say 'sorry' to you."

"Oh? Why?"

He picked at his cuticles. "It was the year before your sister died. The summer I started helping Dad with the lawn." He paused for a second then rushed on. "That time I took a break in the trees by your house. I was young. Stupid. I shouldn't have done it in the first place. I thought I was alone, and then, hearing you two whispering, I should've stopped, and…well…"

Staring at his attractive profile, I saw his neck was glowing red beneath his tan. "What are you talking—" The image bounced into my brain. "Oh! Oooh…"

He risked a glance at me, then snapped back to stare straight ahead. Even his earlobe was crimson.

"You mean the time you…" I moved a loose fist up and down in front of my hips.

"Yeah." His murmur was so soft, I barely heard him.

The look of mortification on such a physically intimidating man was priceless. A giggle escaped. His stunned reaction made me laugh even more. He began snickering along with me. Soon, we were hysterical, both in tears. I had to brace my feet to keep from tumbling over. He got choked up and started to cough. Holding my stomach, I slapped him on the back.

It was a few minutes before we got a hold of ourselves.

"Ah, sweetness," he said when he'd caught his breath. "You're a beautiful surprise."

Tony burst through the door. "Hey, Dad. Dad?" Still chuckling, Bobby looked at his son.

"Yeah, Bubba. What's got you in a tizzy?" He reached up to stroke Tony's cheek.

"Auntie Amber says I got to ask you if I can have some chocolate milk. Can I? Please?"

"Did you have any when you got home from school?"

Tony gravely shook his head. "No. I haven't had none today."

"All right. Half a glass," Bobby replied, a look of

love in his eyes.

Tony jumped in the air with a shout and ran inside.

"And don't—" *Wham!* "—slam the door." Bobby shook his head.

When he turned around, his thigh rested against mine.

"He's a cutie. I can see he's everything to you."

"Yeah, he is," he admitted. "My whole life."

"Do you share custody with his mom?" He pursed his lips at my nosiness. I added, "Never mind. It's none of my business."

"Nah, it's okay. He lives with me full time. But if she thinks I'm drawing attention, she says she'll take him away from me. Fix it so I'll never see him again."

"That's blackmail! Can she do that? Legally, I mean?"

"Sure. She's the mother." He shrugged. "He's always been with me, though. She brought him to me from the hospital after he was born. She lives in Clantonville but never sees him."

Good Lord. She lived in the next town and didn't visit her child? I was curious about who she was, though thought better of prying.

"Does she pay child support?" I asked.

"Nope, never has."

"You should petition the court to give you sole custody. Then she couldn't make threats. If he's always been with you and she's not part of his life, I don't see why it wouldn't be granted. I could check with Zac if you want."

"You think it's possible? I thought mothers had all the say over their kids. Who's Zac?"

"Zac Redondo. He's an attorney in Clantonville.

He handles family cases. Do you want him to call you?"

"He your boyfriend?"

"Yeah. He wants to move to San Antonio to be close to me but had no luck finding a job."

"Oh." His grunt carried a note of disenchantment. "Well, I can't afford a lawyer."

"Nothing wrong with asking. Wouldn't keeping Tony be worth it?"

"Yeah, maybe you're right. Have him call me. I can talk any time after two thirty when I get off work." I dug my phone out of my purse and entered his number.

"Hey, Dad!" Tony interrupted, coming out with a baseball. "Let's play catch. You promised."

"I'm talking to Miss Madisen right now. Remember, you have to wait your turn when someone else is talking."

Tony spun to me. "You wanna play catch?"

I couldn't hide my amusement at Bobby's scowl for being ignored. "How can I resist a handsome young man like you?" I slid my phone into my pocket and climbed to my feet.

I went toward the street side of the small lawn, and Tony stood by the house. As we began tossing the ball, Amber leaned out the door.

"I'm going to take off. See you guys Monday."

Bobby thanked her, and Tony yelled goodbye.

"Nice to meet you, Madisen."

"You, as well," I said. "Thanks for inviting me in." I waved as she drove away.

Bobby and I chatted as I played with Tony. He told me he was fifteen when his father remarried, and they'd moved to Winnser. Bobby had lived in the area ever since. Amber, his stepsister, was seven years older. She took Tony to school and picked him up, staying until Bobby got home from work. His job with a waste management company in the neighboring county explained his physique. Lifting heavy trash cans eight hours a day built a lot of muscle. When I glanced at him, I tried to be discreet. I don't think I was successful, considering the panty-melting smirk he wore.

Bobby stretched out on the porch step, showing off his tightly wrapped body. Occasionally, he gave Tony pointers on catching and throwing. He was too polite to comment on my lack of ability. I found out Tony's aim wasn't great, either. He was tall for a six-year-old and had a strong arm. I had to run into the street to get the balls he fired past me.

Just before dark, I was chasing down another one. Four blocks away, a car screeched around the corner. I stood at the edge of the grass, putting up a hand to shield my eyes from the high beams and waited for it to go by.

But it didn't drive past. Instead, it came straight at me.

Chapter Two

"...Maddie? Wake up, Maddie," Angeline calls from a distance. I'm so deeply asleep, I don't want to be roused. "Maddie, come on. Please." As she persists, her voice becomes louder.

"Huh?" *I mutter.*

"Maddie. You've got to call for help. Hurry..."

Why was there drumming in my skull? After a second, I realized my head, neck, and shoulders pounded with my pulse. I groaned. My arms were heavy as I struggled to move.

A horrible shriek punched through the murkiness in my brain.

Blinking at the terror-filled scream, I looked toward the noise. What I saw got me moving despite the pain.

Red splatters glowed in the slanting light. A small figure howled, kneeling beside a pile of rags. Afraid to stand, I crawled toward the child.

Oh, my God! The heap of cloth was a man splayed on the street. The splashes were blood. It was dripping from his leg as he struggled to lift his head.

The boy turned to me, wailing through his sobs. "Daaah-deeeee!"

Sluggish, the cogs in my mind began to turn. Daddy?

It was Tony. And Bobby.

Before panic could take over, I pulled out my phone. The screen was broken. I dialed Zac, praying the call would go through. When he answered, all I could do was mumble for help. Too queasy to support myself on one hand, I fell to my elbow. I wanted to lie down, but my gut churned, and I threw up.

****

"Ouch!" I said. A strap was pulled snug across my chest.

"Sorry about that. We can't give you anything for the pain yet. You're doing great. Hang in there." The stranger moved into my line of vision. "Can you tell me your name?"

I had to think a second. "It's Madisen."

"Good. What's your last name?"

"Uh, Chandler."

"What day is it?" I couldn't remember. He repeated, "What day of the week is today?"

"Tuesday?" I guessed.

"What town are we in?"

"Clantonville." The man frowned and stepped back, talking into his phone.

"Maddie! Jesus, you scared the shit out of me!" Zac ran to my stretcher. He grabbed my hand and bent to kiss my cheek. I tried to sit up; the strap held me flat.

"My head," I mumbled. "Put it back." I pressed fingers to my ear, hoping to quiet the pounding. A collar had been placed around my neck. I heard a *whump, whump, whump*. It was drawing closer.

"Bobby?" I called. "Get Bobby. He's hurt."

"Shh," Zac said. "He's being treated. The helicopter's coming in. They'll life flight him to the city."

"Tony?"

"He's okay. The police are taking care of him."

I inhaled to say something, then forgot what it was. Instead, I said, "You're mean."

"Why am I mean, baby?" Zac asked, cupping my cheek.

"I don't remember." I admired his strong jaw and tempting mouth. "You're so pretty." I wrinkled my brow. "Where's Tony? He's scared." Zac glanced at the man on the other side of my stretcher.

"You can meet us at the hospital, sir," he said. "We're ready to go."

"I'll see you soon." Zac placed a kiss on my palm and disappeared. As I was being loaded into the ambulance, I noticed another one parked beside it.

I shut my eyes. Since the aches wouldn't let me doze, I gave up and looked around. The stranger sat beside me.

"What happened?" I asked.

"Looks like you landed on your shoulder. Hit your head, too."

I concentrated a minute. "So, what day is it really?"

He gave me a wry smile. "Friday."

We rode the rest of the way in silence.

****

Zac stroked my wrist, holding my hand from a plastic chair by the hospital bed. The ceiling light hurt my eyes, and I squinted at the woman in a lab coat who entered the room. "How are you feeling?" she asked.

"Very well, thank you." One side of her mouth lifted at my rote response. She shined a penlight into my pupils.

"I'm Dr. McGowan. Can you give me your full

name?"

"Madisen Jessica Chandler," I replied.

"And what is today?" She examined me as we talked.

"Friday."

"Good." This time, her grin lit her face and warmed her austere features. She was petite and slender, with a dark ponytail.

"Where are you from?"

"San Antonio. I moved there when I graduated from the University of Missouri."

"What brings you to town?"

Thankful the answer popped into my head, I said, "The wedding. I came to see Jennifer and Jacob get married tomorrow. We were classmates in high school. Oh, the bachelorette party! It's tonight." I winced as she probed another tender spot.

"Okay, Madisen. We're going to do an MRI. You've got deep bruising. It doesn't look like anything's torn or broken. I'll know more about possible neck and head injuries once the results come in."

"Can't the test wait? I don't want to miss Jennifer's last night as a single woman."

"No, you received quite a blow to the head. We need to do it now."

I was helped into a wheelchair by a stout nurse and taken down the hall. With grace, I endured the MRI's thumping in the coffin-like tube, though I felt the fuss was unnecessary.

When I was rolled back to my room, a man was waiting with Zac. I recognized the longish dirty-blond hair and mustache, and the large belly overhanging his belt. I wasn't pleased to see him. When I'd gotten into bed, he offered his hand. "Hello, Madisen."

"Detective," I responded with reservation. My last conversation with John Hanson, the only investigator in the Henry County Sheriff's Department, had been unpleasant. The slow drawl and country-bumpkin appearance concealed his sharp intelligence. The warm manner and amiable expression didn't fool me this time. Without warning, he could change into a callous interrogator. My hesitation must have shown.

"I regret I was hard on you when we talked before. I had to make sure you gave me the whole story. I didn't want any surprises that would benefit your father at his trial." His eyes twinkled.

The apology unknit my conclusion he'd thought I was somehow guilty when I got shot. "Thank you," I said, accepting the handshake.

"I know you've been through a lot," he began, "so I'll keep this brief. Describe what happened."

"I was playing catch with Tony, and he threw the ball past me. I'd started toward the street when a car sped around the corner. I waited for it to pass. Um, I don't recall anything after that. I must've fallen trying to get out of the way."

"Did you see who was driving?"

"No. The lights were too bright. The high beams were on."

"Did you get the license plate? Was it local or out of state?"

"No, I didn't see it."

"What was the make and model?" he asked. I shrugged, flinching. "The color?"

I tried to remember. "Maybe dark blue or

charcoal?"

"Would you be able to identify it if you looked at some pictures?"

"I doubt it. I didn't pay attention. I wasn't in the street and didn't think I'd get hit. It was probably a drunk driver." Detective Hanson didn't acknowledge my assumption, watching me with a blank expression.

I stared at Zac, then back at the detective. The silence grew until it strained the walls. "What's the matter?"

"It could have been…" Zac paused. He stepped close and laced his fingers with mine. "It may have been your father, Maddie."

What? I gaped at Zac. Dread wormed its way into my chest, making my breath stutter.

"We don't know for sure," he added.

"It's only a theory at this point. He's been hiding since the incident in July, and we have no leads regarding his whereabouts," Hanson said, ambling to the door. "We'll look into every possibility. You get some rest. I'll let you know if I have more questions."

I couldn't peel my gaze from Zac. "You haven't told me everything," I said. An image fastened itself to my mind. Tony kneeling in the street. And blood. Lots of it. "Wait. Was Bobby hurt?"

"He pushed you out of the way. He got hit."

He sacrificed himself? To save you? Guilt bloomed inside. "Is he dead?" I whispered, sitting up.

"No! He was flown to the hospital. We'll know more about his condition soon," he said, kissing my lips. "I'm sure he'll be fine. Don't worry, baby. If it was your father driving, he won't get near you. He'll have to go through me first." He pressed me to lie down and pulled the sheet over me.

My father was malicious. I knew that. It wouldn't matter if Zac tried to stop him. He'd find a way to hurt me.

My anxieties were put on hold when Zac's dad, Reynard Redondo, came in. Sheriff Rey had passed his considerable height and Hispanic good looks to his two sons. Although he'd been promoted to corporal, everyone called him "Sheriff" because of his years as a deputy. Zac and his brother Carlos had also inherited his thick black hair, muscular build, and high cheekbones. He kissed my forehead.

"How are you, *mija*?" The endearment, meaning "my daughter," was reassuring.

"It feels like a blood pressure cuff is squeezing my skull." I adjusted the bed to a sitting position. "I guess I'll live."

A smirk split his stoic expression. "Is it worse than the time you drank three bottles of wine and called Zac a 'sasshole'?" he teased.

Rolling my eyes was a mistake. "I didn't drink three bottles by myself. And yes, I'd say this is worse. Do you know how Bobby's doing?"

"They took him to the University Medical Health Center. He went into surgery half an hour ago. They need to find the source of an internal bleed and repair the breaks to his femur. Nothing can be done for his cracked ribs, cuts, and contusions. The good news is there's no sign of brain trauma. The doctors say it's a miracle he doesn't have a head injury from hitting the windshield."

"Oh, God." My heart wedged in my throat. "I feel awful he got hurt saving me." Both men tried to protest.

I cut them off. "Where's Tony? How's he handling it?"

"He's a trouper. He managed to stop crying and remember his aunt Amber's phone number. She came to get him. He couldn't give us any information on the driver or car, though. Before he calmed down, he mentioned another aunt. Maybe the name was Auntie Lane? Do you know who that could be?"

I didn't remember hearing the name. "The only aunt I'm aware of is his auntie Amber."

****

Placed under observation despite my protests, I spent the night in the hospital. Dr. McGowan insisted, even though the MRI was normal. She said another doctor would review the test results in the morning.

Zac couldn't be persuaded to go home. My whole body ached, preventing me from falling asleep, though I'd pretended to. I lay motionless until I was sure Zac had dropped off. Steady breathing came from the chair that was too little for his tall frame. I was afraid he'd slide out of it onto the floor. Dr. McGowan came in hourly, whispering questions. Her visits made it impossible to sleep well after medication had relieved my pain. I guess that was the point.

With half-closed lids, I thought about Bobby's broken body in the street. His injuries were bad. And it was a possibility—no, make that a certainty—my father was out to get me. Again.

Good God Almighty! Remembering made me sit straight up in bed. Angeline had spoken to me, shouting after the accident when I was half conscious, telling me to wake up and get help.

My twin was still with me! She only appeared when I was in my hometown. I thought we'd said our final goodbye at the end of my last visit. A weight lifted, knowing I'd again feel her hugs and hear her laugh. I'd missed talking to her more than I'd expected.

Dread quickly tamped down my joy. My twin sister was murdered a few days after our tenth birthday. We'd begun having conversations a few weeks later while I slept. She had the unnerving ability to predict where I could find lost jewelry, what we'd have for dinner the next day, and when Mother would be too drunk to talk with me after school. Angeline and I had chatted once or twice a week until I left for college. Away from home, she stopped appearing in my dreams. I hadn't returned to Clantonville for a decade and was shocked she spoke to me when I came for a funeral two months ago. I gingerly lay down again and rubbed my temples, wanting to wipe away my unease. Once more, Angeline's presence made me wonder if I was losing my sanity.

Chapter Three

Saturday, September 19

Clinking sounds tickled my ears. I was standing over a nine-year-old classmate, Elaine van Horne, on the playground. Blood smeared her teeth and dripped down her chin. In my dream, I was reliving the day she'd taunted Angeline, calling her prissy.

Unwilling to risk dirtying her new dress, Angeline hadn't joined the games at recess. It didn't take long for Elaine's badgering to strain my nerves. When I whipped around, she must've seen my rage, because she took off. Even though she had a good head start, I easily caught up. Glancing back, she lost her footing and fell hard, hitting her chin on the asphalt. Her bottom teeth cut through the skin under her lip. I hid my satisfaction, pretending alarm as the teachers rushed over.

Accused by Elaine of tripping her, I protested I'd done no such thing. I explained she'd stumbled over her own feet, and when pressed, other children confirmed my story. That angered Elaine even more. It took four stitches to close the cut, and she'd picked at them so much one came out. The resulting scar made Mrs. Van Horne complain her daughter's face would forever be disfigured...

I opened bleary eyes as the memory lingered. It was one of many incidents fueling the intense, mutual dislike between Elaine and me that continued to thrive.

Based on the amount of light coming in the window, I guessed it was midmorning. Zac's chair was empty, and a girl of about eighteen moved around the room. She was plump, with vivid yellow scrubs that matched her hair. She pushed a metal cart holding glass vases, making them ping against one another.

"Well, hello!" she sang when she saw me move.

Ugh. A morning person. "Hello." I yawned, sitting up. My head hurt and I was tired. "What's all this?"

"Get-well wishes. Never seen this many come in so fast." She raised her dark brows.

"You sure they're for me? There're not many people in this town who care enough to send flowers. You must have the wrong room."

"They're all for Madisen Chandler. One says, 'A.K.A. Mad Dash.' That's you, right?" She set the containers around the room.

"Yes," I conceded, smiling at the nickname from my high school track team.

Zac came in holding a paper cup and flashed his beautiful grin, then traced his gaze down to my waist. I was naked under the flimsy hospital gown and could tell what was on his mind. It made me ache for the caress of his lips. I wished we were alone, wanting his satiny skin under my fingers. The direction my thoughts took made me flush. He'd showered, shaved, and wore clean clothes. I inhaled his scent. It reminded me of fresh-cut hay and sunshine.

The perky teenager gawked at him and put on her best simper. It wasn't often women got to be near such a good-looking man. They often took full advantage of it, flirting openly with him. I kept telling myself not to be jealous.

"Hello, there," she cooed.

"Oh," he said, noticing her. "Hi."

The girl left, appearing crestfallen she hadn't received more attention.

"Thanks," I said, reaching out. "Where's yours?"

His eyes crinkled as he surrendered the coffee. "Guess I'll have to share. How are you feeling, gorgeous?" He brushed long fingers up my arm.

I shrugged in answer, blushing at the compliment as I drank. It tasted wonderful.

"Wow," he remarked, taking in the blooms and potted greenery. "I saw these at the front desk not thinking they could all be for you. Do you have other boyfriends?"

"Of course not." I huffed. "It's a mistake. I'm sure some of them are for other patients." I sipped the coffee as he walked around, reading the cards.

"This plant is from Mrs. Wells. These flowers are from Coach Lyons. Liz Snow sent the tulips. The Altar Society of Holy Rosary Church, Delbert and Virginia Tover, Katie and her mom, Charlotte, and Uncle José and Aunt Marie. They're all addressed to you. And the two dozen roses are from me." He handed me one from the vase.

"Oh, Zac! They're beautiful!" I stroked the bud in awe of its perfection. *Wait a minute.* "Are you behind this?"

"Behind what?"

"The flowers. Did you ask everyone to send them?"

"Why would I need to tell people to send you flowers? Is it so hard to believe they want to be nice to you?"

"It's a surprise, is all. I never supposed anyone would be concerned," I said.

"Well, this is proof that lots of folks care."

Tabitha, my best friend since the fifth grade, tornadoed into the room. Zac took a hasty step out of her path. Her boyfriend, Randy Hess, stayed in the hall until she was satisfied I was in one piece.

"My God, Maddie! I was nervous as a whore in church when I heard you got hurt! Are you okay, honey?" she cried, bending down to hug me. Cute as always, she wore a pink sundress and heels that added to her lean five foot seven inches. She had fresh, flawless skin, puppy-dog brown eyes, and a mass of blonde curls trailing down her back.

When she clasped me, I suppressed a groan of pain. She must've heard me wheeze.

"Oh, sorry. I didn't mean to hurt you."

"I'm fine. And happy to see you, too."

"Hey, Dash," Randy said, figuring it was safe to enter.

"Tell me what happened," Tabs demanded before I could answer his greeting.

I gave them a brief rundown of the accident.

When I'd finished, Zac said, "I'm glad you two came by. I want your help. We have a theory it was Maddie's father trying to hurt her again."

Tabs gasped, and Randy stiffened.

"I'd like to get the word out he's in town and might be coming for her. If everyone knows he's back, it'll be harder for him to sneak around."

"Oh, no you don't!" I said, frustration bubbling. "You're not going to spread rumors. It's bad enough the whole town is gossiping about my night in the hospital. No one outside this room needs to know it could've been Father."

"Maddie," Zac warned in that tone. The one he used when his patience was spent.

"No. Absolutely not." Growing up, I'd hated that my alcoholic mother and criminal-defending father drew the disgust of the community. My parents, and me by association, were targeted by local gossips. "I'm not giving ammunition to the rumormongers. I don't object to having Tabs or Randy with me when you have to be at work."

"I already took Thursday and Friday off to spend with her," Tabs said to Zac. "I'll make sure she stays out of trouble."

Zac's snort suggested he didn't think that was possible.

****

Father shook me, cracking my head against the wall. "You will not defy me, Madisen. Ever!" he snarled, spittle hitting my cheek. His violence paralyzed me. I couldn't get enough air into my lungs to scream...

"Time to wake up, Maddie. You need to change for the wedding." Tabs patted my shoulder.

"No," I protested, rolling away. The movement woke me. I jolted, then realized I was in Zac's bedroom. Feeling wrung out when I got home from the hospital, I'd lain down for a nap.

"I figured you wouldn't want to wake up, so I made coffee," Tabs said. Smelling the aroma shut down my nightmare. I pushed myself up and took the cup. After a swallow, I was coherent enough to mumble my thanks.

"You're welcome," she said with a grin. "I know what it takes to get you going."

"Yes, I still worship at the altar of caffeine. Thanks for staying with me, too. And for your help bringing the flowers." I'd been a little surprised when she'd insisted we keep every single one. I was okay with leaving a plant or two at the hospital for others to enjoy.

"You are more than welcome." She was beaming.

"Okay," I said, narrowing my eyes, "what aren't you telling me?" She wouldn't, would she? "Oh, no. Please do not say everyone sent flowers because you blabbed I was in the hospital. You, of all people!"

She tried to look offended. "No, I did not tell everybody."

"Yeah, riiight."

"Well, after Zac called last night, I just happened to mention to Mrs. Wells you'd had an accident and were in Clantonville Memorial."

"Tabs!" I whined. "Mrs. Wells is a notorious busybody. You might as well announce it on the radio."

"Oh, don't be so dramatic. I didn't give her details, and everyone would've found out anyway. Mrs. Wells is such a sweet lady. She was worried for you. And she didn't hold a gun to their heads and force people to send you flowers. Everyone was happy as a dead pig in sunshine to do it."

I gazed at her in confusion. She'd lived in Alabama until she was ten, and I thought I'd heard all her sayings, what I called her "Southern-isms." But this one left me blank.

She drawled, "You know, when the old sow dies in the mud hole, the sun's heat shrinks up the skin. It pulls back from her teeth, giving her a big ol' smile."

"Ick." I shuddered. "I could've gone forever without that image in my head."

Tabs scrunched her cute nose and handed me a bottle of pain relievers. I took two and slogged to the shower. Zac was due home from the office, and Tabs would leave when he arrived.

****

The evening air was humid. Bees puttered among the park's dandelions. I shifted in my seat, trying to displace a sturdy straw poking me from the hay bale we sat on. Rows of square bales formed an aisle leading to a small trellis. Artificial flowers covered the top of the arch.

My body ached, and the uncertainties rattling around my head made me restless. With Father in town, how would I protect myself? I thought about discussing it with Detective Hanson or Sheriff Rey. I discarded the idea, knowing they'd tell me to let them handle it. I couldn't accept being left defenseless. In my mind, I pictured Father and his evil expression. I couldn't get the image out of my head.

Zac noticed my fidgeting and pulled me close, brushing his lips over my temple. I nuzzled his jaw and inhaled his scent. He growled when I nipped him. "Be good," he whispered. Thankful for his support, I knew I couldn't survive if he weren't by my side.

The music grew louder. The minister, groom, and three groomsmen lined up in front. They wore black suit jackets, black jeans, cowboy boots, and black hats. Except for Jacob. His Stetson was white, held snug by a chin strap, and he looked skinny under its broad brim. I imagined the wind turning it into a kite and carrying him over the trees.

The bridesmaids walked quickly down the aisle. They wore yellow and purple floral prairie dresses with puffed three-quarter sleeves, fitted bodices, and gathered skirts. The hems ended four inches from the ground, showing plenty of lilac boot. Zac's snicker ended in a quiet "Oomph" when my elbow connected with his ribs.

"Aren't they lovely?" I whispered. He raised one eyebrow, then nodded, seeing my glower. He must not have known the unwritten rule. The wedding party had to endure the bride's abuse of good taste to guarantee no one would outshine her. They needed all the encouragement they could get.

A little girl about four years old walked hesitantly down the aisle. A tiny version of the dress and purple boots was cute on her. She was determined to keep both hands latched onto the handle of her white basket. From the first row, her mother urged her to drop petals. She refused, perhaps wanting them as a prize for surviving the gauntlet.

Everyone stood when the wedding march began. Jennifer exuded happiness in her white strapless dress with a voluminous skirt. It suited her roundish figure. She carried a massive bouquet, and a wreath of yellow flowers crowned her auburn hair. Attached was a long veil trailing in the grass with fluttering white ribbons. I glanced at Jacob. Catching sight of her, he got a dreamy expression, then broke into an elated grin.

The minister opened with his impressions of the bride and groom. In his years counseling couples, he'd not seen one who brought out the best in each other as much as Jennifer and Jacob. They exemplified a union that was greater than the sum of its parts.

The ceremony was charming. I tried to concentrate, not wanting to disrespect my friends. I couldn't seem to corral my nerves. At least the ritual was short, finishing in twenty minutes. I hoped a glass of wine at the reception would slow my runaway thoughts.

****

The park's community building was utilitarian green metal on the outside. Inside, the linoleum floors were scuffed to the color of dust. Accordion partitions were folded away to form one large room. Bargain silk flowers decorated the white paper tablecloths with purple-and-yellow crepe paper draped around the edge. We found seats with my high school classmate Katie and her mother, Charlotte.

Katie was a loyal friend. Always animated, her pageboy hairstyle swung with energy. In her job as a teacher, she easily kept up with her second-grade students. She had a two-year-old son, Ty, who was absent from the reception.

Charlotte was sixtyish, a graying version of her daughter. Her brown eyes creased when she saw me.

"Thank you so much for the flowers," I said.

"You're welcome, Dash," Katie answered.

Charlotte fired questions at me, leaning forward in her seat. "We're glad you came. Are you feeling better? We heard you suffered a blow to the head. What happened?"

I had a lie all prepared, knowing people would want details. Remembering Elaine's childhood accident, I explained, "When I was running, I glanced back and stumbled. I bruised my shoulder and hit my head on a rock. I have a mild concussion. It'll heal up in no time." I stared pointedly at Zac, who shook his head at me.

"Oh, I'm glad it's not too serious. Isn't this a lovely wedding?" Katie practically salivated. A single mother, she was on the lookout for a man who was husband material. Believing everyone should take a nosedive into matrimony, she shifted her attention to Zac and me. I cut her off before she got any bright ideas.

"It's very pretty. I know it took Jennifer months to put together. Thank goodness I won't ever have to do it." Zac's expression turned sour. Rubbing my neck, I asked, "Sweetie, would you mind getting me a glass of wine?" As Randy and Tabs approached, he stalked off in silence. *What's gotten into him?*

Tabs looked beautiful in a slinky, pale-green dress. She'd moved to town the summer Angeline died. We met on her first day of school when she rejected Elaine's claim I'd drowned my twin out of jealousy. Tabitha always had my back, fiercely defending me against detractors. She'd been living with Randy for over a year, and I was pretty sure they'd get engaged soon. He was the salt of the earth, a truly nice person. A perfect counterpoint to Tabs's liveliness, he was easygoing, with a goatee, shaggy hair, and a small gap between his front teeth. A bit itchy in his suit and tie, he looked handsome, nonetheless.

Saying hello to Katie and Charlotte, Tabs sat in the chair beside me. "Don't you look cute," she said.

I'd worn a short-sleeved dress with a fitted bodice and swishy skirt falling just above the knee. It was teal, bringing out the blue in my eyes. "Thanks. And you look fabulous."

"Thank you. Have you noticed Elaine?" Tabs

asked. "I've never seen her this withdrawn. She's sitting at the table, hunched over, not looking at anyone. Mrs. Van Horne is trying not to be obvious, but I can tell she's watching her like a hawk. Hell's gonna freeze over if they don't stick their noses so high in the air they could drown in a rainstorm."

This stirred my interest. Elaine and her mother, Caroline, felt it was their responsibility to set the example of propriety. They'd normally work the room, showily greeting their friends. The Van Hornes pretended to be models of social decorum, though everyone knew they spread vicious gossip. They never let a single person forget they had a spotless reputation.

"That's strange. Wonder what's up with her?" I mused.

"What's up with who?" Zac asked, rejoining us.

"Elaine," Tabs answered. "She and Caroline seem to have misplaced their 'superiority capes.' And Elaine hasn't even made one hateful remark to Maddie."

"Yeah, it was odd she didn't speak to me when I passed her," Zac said.

"There you go! Proof something's going on," Tabs insisted.

I let out a bitter huff. Elaine didn't miss a chance to remind me of my sister's death. Nor had she accepted that Zac was now my boyfriend. They'd stopped dating a year ago, and she was determined to recapture his attention. I wouldn't have put it past her to hog-tie and drag him down the aisle when the minister was handy. After she found out Zac and I were in a relationship, her hatred of me swelled to colossal proportions.

We glanced at them, seeing Elaine lean over to speak in her mother's ear. Caroline shook her head.

Elaine whispered again, and Caroline's expression turned ghastly. Elaine winced when Caroline grabbed her arm and marched her across the room, heels tapping a quick rhythm.

Gwendolyn Hayes tried to talk to them and was ignored. "Well, I never!" Mrs. Hayes said to Caroline's back. Everyone along their path watched as the Van Hornes clacked out and slammed the door.

"Hellfire!" Tabs muttered as we stared, gaping.

Zac set a soda on the table, breaking our trance.

"They aren't serving wine?" I asked.

"The doctor said you can't drink alcohol with a concussion." I gave him my best pout. He chuckled, and I couldn't stay mad at him. His rich laugh healed me like a tonic.

Chapter Four

After the two hundred and fifty guests were seated, the DJ introduced the newlyweds. Everyone cheered when they entered. Since the tableware was plastic, the guests couldn't clink the glasses to demand a public display of affection, but shouts of "Kiss! Kiss!" went up. A big smooch by the bride and groom ended the catcalls. Jacob thanked everyone for coming and invited us to enjoy the buffet, kegs of beer, and bottles of wine.

We were standing in line for the fantastic-smelling brisket, baked beans, and potato salad when I lurched into Zac. My father stood across the room in a navy suit that complemented his silver hair. When the man turned, I saw he was a stranger.

Zac steadied me, putting his lips to my ear. "Try to relax. I don't think your father will show up with so many people here." His breath, then his warm tongue, caressed my neck. His effort to distract me worked. I pictured him pinning me against the bathroom wall, my legs wrapped around his waist. I unbuttoned his pants as he pushed up my dress. I blinked to clear the image. It still surprised me how easily he stirred my lust.

I noticed Zac wasn't following his own advice. He continually surveilled the crowd. Tabs was sticking close, as well. She'd already bumped into me and stepped on my shoe. Their tension was catching, and I struggled to remain calm by breathing deeply. I was thankful Zac and Randy had martial arts training and quick reactions. Still, black belts weren't bulletproof vests, and I already carried the responsibility for Bobby's injuries. I had to find a way to keep the people I cared about safe if my father started shooting.

As we drew toward the buffet table, Jan and Mike Owens, Virginia and Delbert Tover, and April Overfeld waved or nodded and whispered to their neighbors. I could tell they were dying to get the scoop about my hospital stay. In addition to the wedding, it was a notable event in the small town.

We ate our meal quickly, even though the *Clantonville News* reporter Jayce Phelps interrupted us. I again explained I'd fallen while jogging, omitting the fact I was injured in Winnser. To my relief, Phelps didn't make the connection to Bobby's accident or ask further questions. Resigned to being the subject of a short article, I knew a lie printed in the paper was better than the truth coming out.

Before the speeches and toasts started, Zac and I went to congratulate the newlyweds. Jennifer was feeding Jacob a forkful of beans. After he took a bite, they rubbed noses, absorbed in each other. I interrupted them and told the fib about tripping during my run. Begging their forgiveness for leaving early, I explained my aches made it impossible to stay. They were concerned and wished me a quick recovery. We took a picture of the four of us, then Zac and I made our escape.

****

Sunday, September 20

...By the wading pond at Father's house, I lean back on my elbows and dig my toes in the sand. He'd

put the sand in to keep the mud back when we splashed in the shallow water. After Angeline died, I seldom came here. It was too painful a reminder that she was gone.

Infinite stars prick the clear sky, and the quarter moon is peeking over the trees. Cool drops of water flick my arm, and I hear Angeline laugh.

I jump up and pull her into a hug. "It's so good to see you! I was afraid I'd never talk to you again."

Joy lights her beautiful face, which will forever be that of a ten-year-old. Seeing her almost makes me cry.

"Hi, Maddie," she says, laying a palm on my cheek. She gives me a searching look, then settles on the blanket beside me.

At a loss, I'm not sure how to start. "I'm sorry I haven't done anything yet to make Father pay for what he did. The—"

"Let's not talk about Mommy and Daddy. I want to talk about the rest of us."

"The rest of who?" I ask.

"The ones who love you. Especially the new one."

"Well, it's going better with Zac than I thought it might. Talking on the phone isn't the same as seeing him every day. He interviewed with two firms in San Antonio and came home. He didn't get a job offer, so he's still looking. I guess we'll try to maintain the relationship long distance. I'm not sure what else we can do."

She says, "No, I didn't mean him."

"Who are you talking about?"

She starts to speak, decides not to, and looks at me wistfully. Then she stares in silence at the smooth water. An owl hoots in the distance. After a pause, she says, "The ones who hate you won't stop. You have to be careful..."

Wakefulness came in a rush. I was alone in bed and stretched my arms wide. Last night, Zac had politely declined my invitation to make love, saying he wouldn't chance jarring my head. Apparently, he'd spoken to the doctor in private about activities banned for people with concussions. "Scream-like-a-banshee, wild-as-a-rodeo, put-you-in-a-bliss-coma sex," he'd said, "tops the list of things you cannot do."

Protesting hadn't gotten him to budge, and I'd fallen asleep in his arms faster than expected.

In a drowsy haze, I remembered my talk with Angeline. *The new one who loves you.* If not Zac, then who did she mean? She'd also said people wouldn't stop hating me, and I did know who they were. My father, of course. Also, Elaine van Horne and her mother, Caroline. Those two were chairwomen of the "We Hate Maddie Chandler" club. They wouldn't end their crusade of scorn during my lifetime, so I didn't understand why Angeline had mentioned it. I wondered briefly about Elaine's odd behavior at the wedding last evening.

It was just one more worry skittering around my head like dried leaves in a gale.

To halt the internal dialogue, I got up to take a shower. I really wished I could go for a run. Pounding the pavement for an hour would let my mind work through the stress. I usually ran every other day; it was my self-prescribed anti-anxiety drug.

Zac would probably lock me in the house if I even suggested jogging today.

Under a shower spray as hot as I could stand, I

heard the bathroom door open and close. Peeking around the curtain, I saw a cup of coffee on the vanity. *Aww, that man knows the way to your heart.*

Zac lived in a rented two-bedroom, one-bath, ranch-style house. The front door was between the beige living room on the right and the dining area on the left with the kitchen behind it. The hall ran straight back to the bathroom and bedrooms. It was sparsely furnished with secondhand items except for the huge TV and black leather couch. A typical bachelor pad, he kept it neat and casual.

By the time I'd dressed and dried my hair, he'd fixed a breakfast of scrambled eggs with sausage, potatoes, and toast. His good morning hug and kiss were beyond distracting. I forced myself to pull away and sat at the table. When he brought the food and joined me, I listlessly stared at my plate.

"It's unusual for you not to eat," he said.

"Thanks for going to the trouble. It's good. I'm just not very hungry."

"Something on your mind?"

"I'd rather not discuss it," I said.

"I would feel better if you talked to me, Maddie."

At times, he complained I didn't trust him enough to tell him everything. I found the remark irritating. I wasn't ready to reveal my deepest secret that I talked to Angeline.

Maybe it was time to apply the new personal rule. Being open about my fears went against my nature, yet I saw the logic in it. I was willing to take a baby step, hoping he'd be satisfied with a tiny piece of the truth.

"Being home makes me think of Mother," I said, putting down my cup. Five years ago, she'd tried to kill herself with pills and alcohol. She'd suffered slight brain damage from oxygen deprivation and lived in a nursing home. Though psychiatric tests were inconclusive, doctors suspected a mental disorder because Mother believed she conversed with Angeline. If that meant she was insane, then I was too.

"What are you worried about?"

"More like terrified." I realized too late I'd said it out loud.

"You're not planning to visit her, are you?" When I shook my head, he asked, "Why are you scared?"

I didn't answer, letting the question hang between us. Chancing a peek at him, I saw he was squinting in concentration.

"You'll never end up like her, you know."

His words hit me like a nuclear detonation. "What did you say?"

"It's not uncommon for people to be afraid they'll repeat their parents' mistakes. I am." He took a bite of eggs and gestured with his fork. "From what you've told me, your mother was emotionally unstable long before Angeline died. I think remorse for what she did finally pushed her over the edge. You're not burdened by that kind of guilt. You have no reason to be afraid you'll attempt to take your own life."

Holy smokin' guacamole! His statement shocked me more than if the house had been carried to the land of Munchkins. My mouth hung open. I clacked it shut.

I'd assumed Angeline's voice was the sole reason for Mother's instability. But could she have been mentally ill before Angeline died? And was her suicide attempt the result of guilt added to her burden of all-consuming grief?

I stared at Zac as he ate. He had no clue he'd addressed the fundamental root of my fears. I sat quietly, letting the idea percolate. It would need a lot of thought. "Wow." I looked at him from the corner of my eye. "Have you been talking to my headshrinker?" I joked.

He chuckled. "Your 'headshrinker'? Is that what you call your therapist?"

"Yeah. What you said could've come straight from her. Should I call you Dr. Zac Smarty-pants?"

"No, I'm not a psychology expert. However, there is something in my pants I can use with a high level of expertise. We have to wait two more days," he said with a delightful leer.

"Two days, huh? We could start getting warmed up right now. Can you survive forty-eight hours of foreplay without cracking?"

"If I wasn't expecting company, I'd take you up on the offer."

"Who's coming over?" I asked.

"Lauren should be here any minute." Zac hadn't known his half sister existed until ten weeks ago. They'd met at the funeral of his aunt Ceci, who was also my surrogate mother. Lauren had come to the burial with his mother, Deborah. And he hadn't seen or heard from Deborah for thirty years. Pregnant with Lauren, she'd vanished from Zac's life shortly before his first birthday. Lauren was eighteen months older than me and had a cute little girl named Grace.

"You should've let me know," I said, taking my plate to the kitchen. "I'll see if Tabs wants to go shopping so you two can have some privacy."

"I'm not letting you go shopping," he said, slipping

behind me at the sink. "Not when it's possible your father's out there. Besides, she made a point to come while you're here. She wants to get acquainted with you."

That surprised me since Zac hadn't even gotten to know her yet. He'd been conflicted about being a part of her and Grace's life because he thought Sheriff Rey would be against it. Apparently, he'd made the decision to do so. And hadn't told me.

Guess you're not the only one holding things back.

****

When he answered the doorbell, Zac invited Lauren in. She had a lighter complexion than Zac but shared his high forehead and straight nose. Like her mother, she was ash blonde, and tall and slender. Attractive, with a friendly manner. She greeted me with an easygoing embrace. I couldn't put my finger on why I felt an immediate rapport with her.

Zac fixed her a glass of iced tea as she sat with me on the sofa, then pulled up a chair from the dining table.

"I'm so happy to meet you, Maddie. I hope you've recovered?" Lauren asked. We hadn't been introduced at Aunt Ceci's burial or the next week when she'd mysteriously shown up with Father at his house right before our confrontation. I owed her a debt of gratitude I didn't know how to repay. As Father had shot at me, she'd grabbed his arm and ruined his aim. I was hit just above my right hip instead of between the eyes.

"Oh, yes, I'm fine. Thanks for asking. The bullet wound healed fast. I don't know how to thank you for saving my life. If you hadn't been there, I'd be dead. Two little words aren't enough."

"Hearing you say them is enough, and you're

welcome," she said. "Zac and I have talked some on the phone, and he's told me a little about you. You live in San Antonio?"

"Yes, it's been six years now. A few weeks after I moved, I started working for a big insurance company there. I handle customer service for auto, homeowners, and renters policies."

"That's interesting." A spark of curiosity lit her face. "I got a job with a title company nine months ago, doing closings for homebuyers. I don't understand why the insurance policy doesn't always cover the loan amount."

I explained that the mortgage amount could vary due to lot size or the amount of the down payment. The homeowner's policy, designed to protect the structure, was based on the estimated cost to rebuild. We talked about our careers, then moved on to personal topics. I learned she was dedicated to yoga and practiced four times a week. I explained, despite the yoga pants I wore, I'd never tried it. While I made a point to work out with weights, my true addiction was running. She looked at me like I'd lost my mind. She avoided the "dreadmills" at her fitness club, calling them torture devices.

She chatted about her daughter, telling us how mischievous Grace was. Her kindergarten teacher had called last week. "Grace had swallowed a nickel at recess because the other kids asked to look at it. Her daddy told her not to lose it, and Grace thought if it was in her tummy, no one could take it." She sighed in annoyance. "It's been a week, and it hasn't passed through her system. I took her to get an X-ray Friday, and it didn't show up. Matthew thinks it's hilarious.

When we got home from the clinic, he asked if there was any *change* in the shit-uation."

Zac and I laughed at the irritated look on Lauren's face as much as her husband's joke.

"Pretty smart of her," I said when I could speak again.

"Too smart for her own good. She gets her impish side from Matthew."

We sat in comfortable silence a moment. Then Zac revealed I'd spent Friday night in the hospital. Visibly shaken, Lauren asked if I would mind sharing what happened.

Before I could give her my made-up story, Zac said, "Someone tried to run her down with a car. Thank God the guy she was visiting pushed her out of the way. I'm afraid the driver might've been her father."

"You're kidding!" Lauren's hand flew to her chest. "He's still hiding to avoid arrest, isn't he? Do you think he'd risk getting caught just to hurt you?"

"Yes, I think he'd chance it. He's determined to get revenge for my threat to put him in prison." I frowned at Zac. "I'd appreciate it if you wouldn't tell anyone. I'm not comfortable with it getting out. Promise?"

"Oh, of course I won't," Lauren said. "You can depend on it. I consider you family, too."

Whew! Though I barely knew her, I trusted her to keep her word.

"I'm hungry," Zac announced. "You want to join us for lunch, Lauren?"

"Gosh. I had no idea it was so late. I've got to get home to Grace and Matthew. They've probably booby-trapped the house by now." When I got to my feet, she laid her hands on my shoulders and searched my face.

"Please be careful, Maddie. We don't want to lose you, and I know how dangerous your father is." She gave me a long hug goodbye, waved at Zac, and hurried out.

Before he'd turned the dead bolt, Lauren tapped on the door. "I hope you don't think I'm paranoid," she said. "There's a car down the block, parked in the same spot as when I came. Someone's still sitting inside."

"You two stay here," Zac ordered. Before I knew it, he'd run out, shutting the door behind him. I stared at the insubstantial wood barrier.

It seemed we waited an eternity. Wondering what was taking so long, I imagined him on the ground, stare fixed, with a tidy hole in his forehead. I was about to reach for the knob when he walked in.

"They took off as soon as they saw me coming. I didn't see who was driving. The license plate was smeared with mud. I couldn't get a look at the number."

No! I was sure it had to be Father, looking for another opportunity. Nausea slicked my stomach, and I sank to the arm of the couch.

"Maddie? You okay?" Zac held me by the arms.

"Yeah, f-fine," I faltered. He pulled me up and helped me sit on the cushions. Lauren brought me a glass of water.

"You're awfully pale. You sure you're okay?" Zac asked. I nodded. "All right. I'll walk Lauren to her car. Be right back."

A minute later, he sat close and collected me in his arms. I burrowed into his side, trying to get even nearer. An avalanche of helplessness threatened to bury me.

Keeping one arm tight around my shoulders, he pulled out his phone. "Hi, Detective, this is Zac Redondo. You know Maddie's staying with me, right? I wanted to tell you someone was watching the house from a car down the street." He paused, listening. "I couldn't see. It was a gray coupe, newer model. The plate was covered with mud. It looks kind of familiar, but I can't place it." Another pause, and he hung up. "He's letting Dad know."

Five minutes later, his phone rang. "Hi, Dad." He repeated his conversation with Detective Hanson word for word, except he listened longer.

When he hung up, he said, "Dad's asking for volunteers from the department to help. With one or two others, he and Hanson should be able to put a plainclothes watch on the house for the next thirty-six hours."

"I hate to cause this much trouble."

"Baby, you aren't causing it. Your father is. And people want to help. They'll be glad to do it." It was nice to hear, though I didn't believe him. "Dad gave me an update on Bobby's condition."

That pulled me out of my self-pity. "How is he?"

"The internal bleeding was from a ruptured spleen. They removed it and realigned his femur by putting a rod inside. The bone had punctured the leg muscles in two places, so he'll need physical therapy. He's out of ICU, and his prognosis is good. There's still no sign of head trauma, and doctors will probably let Detective Hanson interview him in the morning."

Responsibility dragged me down like concrete shoes. I thought of Tony. *My God, Madisen. What have you done?* "And if his leg doesn't heal properly?"

"Stop," Zac said. I looked at him, eyes wide. "I can tell you're blaming yourself. None of this is your fault."

"Bobby wouldn't be hurt if I hadn't been there.

How can it not be my fault?"

"It's not like you're the one who ran him down. You weren't planning for him to get hurt."

I heaved a sigh.

"Listen," he continued, "you aren't responsible for other people's actions."

"You sound like my therapist again."

"Well," he said, scratching his arm, "that's because I've spent a fair amount of time with one."

"Seriously? When?"

"Don't look so shocked. When I was in college, I dated a girl who was a psychology major. To make a long story short, she said I had abandonment issues because Mom left when I was a toddler. It took a lot to swallow my pride and see a counselor. I went to him for three years. It helped me get my head on straight and recognize what I was doing wrong."

"Oh my God! That's why you made the comment about the mistakes of our parents," I said. "So, you were afraid of being abandoned?"

"Yes, and the way I acted made it inevitable. Without realizing it, I alienated women because I was insecure."

"What do you mean?"

"I did things like showing up late or not at all. Flirting with other girls in front of my date. I pushed them away by being an ass. Subconsciously, I wanted them to be loyal. To stay with me despite my behavior. Prove I was worthy. But people can only be pushed so far before they give up. I forced them to leave.

"Once the counselor figured out my issues, he said I had to be aware of my motives, analyze my actions, and manage my expectations. It was hard at first. It got easier with practice. And I kept at it."

He'd spent three years with a therapist? Huh. No wonder he was able to give such good advice.

My perception of Zac began to change. I'd always viewed him as perfect. Knowing he'd struggled with personal issues and conquered them made me admire him even more.

And it made me think of the emotional baggage I carried. My shoulders sagged.

"What's wrong?" he asked. I couldn't answer. "Maddie?" His tone made me look up.

"I— It's just…" There was nothing left to lose at this point. Wrinkling my nose, I said, "In one of my therapy sessions, I learned I have a fear of commitment. Why would you want to be with someone like me?"

His response to this new complication wasn't what I anticipated. He tapped the end of my nose and kissed it. "You're the toughest, most resilient person I know, and the only woman I want. We'll be fine."

Chapter Five

Six o'clock that evening found us waiting for Zac's dad, brother, aunt, uncle, and cousins to arrive. Since I was a child, they'd welcomed me as a member of the family. Aunt Marie was bringing dinner. I'd been looking forward to her Tex-Mex cooking since I'd gotten to town. It was better than I could get in San Antonio. I wiped my mouth to be sure I hadn't drooled.

"So, what did you think of Lauren?" Zac was trying too hard to sound casual.

"About that," I said. "Why didn't you say you'd decided to get to know her? I thought you were worried about upsetting your dad."

Zac hesitated, and my stomach dropped. Why was he being secretive?

"Other things are—" he started. There was a knock at the door.

The tide that was the Redondo clan poured in. Chaos filled Zac's small living room as seven people talked at once. Linda Marie, Zac's cousin, had corralled her frizzy mop into a pretty up-do that enhanced her features. She stuck to my side with an arm around my waist, her head resting on my shoulder. She blinked away the moisture in her eyes.

Her sister Teresa, and Teresa's husband, Joshua, reached around Linda Marie to hug me. After Uncle José and Aunt Marie set the covered dishes they carried on the table, they clasped me like I'd died and come back to life. Eventually, Zac's older brother Carlos pushed them aside and pressed every scrap of air from my lungs. Then came Sheriff Rey.

"*Mija*," he said, touching my cheek. The understanding and support of his simple endearment made my throat close. He kissed my head and wrapped his strong arms around me like a beloved daughter.

"Sit," commanded Uncle José when Sheriff Rey released me. Shorter than his brother, Uncle José was also rounder and more jovial.

I obediently plopped on the sofa as Carlos and Josh went to get more food from the car.

"Tell us everything," Uncle José continued. "How did you get hurt? The girls only knew that you tripped when you were running. Are you okay?"

"Yes, I'm fine. And thank you for sending flowers." I was grateful Sheriff Rey was the only one aware of what had really happened. As an officer in the sheriff's department, he couldn't contradict my lie by revealing details about an open investigation. "There's not much to tell. I fell and hit my head. I called Zac, and we went to Clantonville Memorial. No injuries showed up on the tests. I only stayed overnight because the doctor insisted due to a mild concussion. It'll resolve in a couple of days."

"*Gracias a Dios*," Uncle José said.

Yeah, thank God they believe you. I felt horrible for being dishonest. Yet, if they knew the truth, they might get hurt trying to protect me. I couldn't live with myself if one of them were injured.

"It's great to hear you'll be fine. We were afraid there were complications from your bullet wound,"

Linda Marie said.

"No, it wasn't that," I answered. "And I learned my lesson. In the future, I promise I'll contact you if there's a serious issue."

"What a relief," Teresa said, taking one of the dishes from Josh. "Okay, let's eat. I'm starving."

Confident I wouldn't shut them out again, they mobbed the overloaded table. No one noticed my smile was forced. I had stooped to disloyalty, knowing how much it would hurt them. *You're such a hypocrite, Madisen.*

I stole a look at Sheriff Rey, who hadn't joined the rush to fix a plate. He refused to glance in my direction. I burned with shame at the rebuke.

Everyone congregated in the living room, sitting on the sofa and floor. I dug into the tamales, black beans, rice, homemade salsa, and fried zucchini. I wished Aunt Marie could move in with me so I could eat like this all the time. To keep from becoming a blimp, though, I'd have to run a hundred miles a day.

"This is so good, Aunt Marie. How do you do it? Each meal tastes better than the last," I said around the food I was chewing.

Uncle José ran a hand down his wife's black hair. "That's why I keep her around. She feeds me." His Pancho Villa mustache puffed out when she smacked his head. Everyone snickered at his startled look.

"That's not the only reason," she said.

"No. The fact you're the love of my life is probably important too." He gave her a lingering kiss, and Teresa covered her eyes.

"Gah," she said. "You two need to learn some boundaries. No public displays of affection!"

The Art of Being Broken

Uncle José guffawed, and we giggled.

"Maddie, I brought the tax and utility bills for Aunt Ceci's house. Well, your house, I mean," Carlos said, handing me the mail.

"I'll always think of it as Aunt Ceci's house," I said. Sheriff Rey and Uncle José's sister, Cecilia, had left me her property. During my visit to attend her funeral, the inside was trashed in a random act of vandalism. Carlos and Josh had been a huge help, throwing the damaged items away. They'd also covered the graffiti and begun refinishing the spray-painted floors.

I thumbed through the bills. I'd already paid them online, so I stuffed them in my pocket.

"As soon as you feel up to it," Carlos said, slinging an arm around Josh, "you can take a look at the work we've done." The bump made Josh's fork miss his mouth, and he poked his chin. "Not to brag, but it's looking pretty good."

"I can't wait to see it."

"Maddie needs a few more days to recover," Sheriff Rey said. "I'm sure she'll get over there before she leaves." I assumed he wanted to keep me tucked indoors while my father was a threat.

"Thanks to both of you for all your work," I said, patting Carlos's arm. "I wish you would let me pay you."

"No need. I've made a point to go shirtless when I'm outside," Carlos said, flexing a bicep. "Two women asked me out. Compensation received."

Josh shook his head.

"Huh?" Linda Marie twitched at the chance to tease him. "I thought you were hung up on that girl

Andie you met at the lake. Aren't you fixing her SUV? And who in their right mind would date you? Give me their numbers. I'll warn them off."

Carlos lunged at her, napkins and plastic utensils flying. He hoisted her petite frame over his shoulder with a playful slap on the rear.

"What? What?" she yelped, giggling.

"Repeat after me," he said. "Carlos is a godsend to women, and I'm honored to bask in his handsomeness."

She reiterated his words, the last one sounding suspiciously like "ass-ishness." He set her on her feet with a final swat.

An idea struck me amid the laughter. I knew money was tight for Teresa and Josh. He'd been laid off a month ago, and his search hadn't landed a job yet. The handyman work he picked up locally didn't bring in much. "Teresa, don't you two want to get out of your apartment? Why don't you move in?"

They both looked hopeful, then Teresa's expression fell. "We can't afford the rent on a house. We appreciate the offer, though."

"Who said you'd pay rent? It'd be a load off my mind to have tenants who'll take good care of it."

Everyone looked at Teresa. "We can't take advantage of you like that."

Heads swiveled my way. "What's the payment on your apartment?" I asked.

"The place is tiny and a total dump. The landlord's lucky to get the three hundred we cough up. It's not even worth that."

"It's a deal."

Eyes ping-ponged to her.

"No way," she shot back.

"Two hundred. That's my final offer."

"You're supposed to ask for more, not less!"

"You two can pay the utilities. They're probably high since it's an older home," I countered. "I couldn't stand it if I end up with tenants that would neglect or even damage it. Please? You two love the house as much as I do. I wouldn't have to hire a management company, so it'll save me their fees. Say you'll do it."

Teresa started to waver, and Josh looked at his wife hopefully.

"Okay, we'll move in!" she said. "We'll notify our landlord."

"Yes!" Josh hugged her.

They didn't need to know I never intended to cash their rent checks.

When midnight rolled around, Zac resorted to shooing the family out, correctly telling them I was tired and needed my rest. My cheeks ached from laughing, and I hadn't thought of my father the whole evening. *What would you do without that family?*

As I yawned, Zac guided me into the bedroom and pulled my top off, taking care not to hurt my sore shoulder.

Ooh, this could get interesting.

He unhooked my bra and dropped it to the floor, placing a string of kisses from my neck to my shoulder.

I closed my lids with a hum but opened them when he tugged a clean T-shirt over my head. *Damn.* I was hoping he'd forgotten his promise to wait until Tuesday and stuck my bottom lip out.

"I know. I don't like it either," he said, touching my temple. "We're not taking a chance your beautiful brain will get hurt."

"Okay," I said in a huff. "I'll sleep on the air mattress in the other room."

"Oh, no, you don't. Just because we can't make love doesn't mean I don't want your body next to mine."

I couldn't hide my satisfaction as we cuddled close for the night.

****

Monday, September 21

At 9:23, I bolted out of bed, thinking it would already be too hot for my run. The movement made my head pound and reminded me I wouldn't be jogging today. At least the pain wasn't as bad as yesterday.

Listening carefully, I heard the TV in the living room. I meandered down the hall and saw Zac sitting at the kitchen table bent over his laptop. Not wanting to disturb him, I crept into the kitchen, tempted by the aroma of coffee. I got a cup as Zac wrapped his arms around me. Too groggy to be startled, I sank against his hard body. "Good morning," I murmured.

"Good morning to you." He kissed behind my ear. *Boy, you could get used to that every day.* "How are you doing?"

"I still ache a little. Maybe moving around will help the stiffness." I didn't pull away. His solid dependability felt too good.

After two short minutes of nuzzling my hair, he said, "I'd better go back to work before I get carried away." He sat down, and I took my cup to the bedroom.

My heart hit bottom when I remembered Detective Hanson would talk to Bobby today. If his doctors approved.

Throughout the morning, I had to remind myself to

breathe. After wasting as much time as I could stretching and doing easy exercises, I took a long shower. I dressed and sat in the living room, trying not to fidget as I read a magazine.

Why hadn't Sheriff Rey called to let us know what Bobby had told the detective?

Zac must have noticed my disquiet. "You hungry?" he asked.

"A little." I walked to him, combing his hair with my fingers. "I can fix you lunch, if you want to keep working."

"No, thanks. I need a break. This contract research is making my eyes cross. I'd much rather look at you." He gave me a peck on the cheek, went to the kitchen, and pulled the makings for a cold sandwich out of the fridge.

I followed to get a glass of iced tea and watched him assemble a gargantuan double-decker with three kinds of meats, two types of cheese, bacon, lettuce, tomato, and mustard.

"You'd better let me make my own. I'd have to unhinge my jaw to eat that," I said.

"This is a masterpiece." He gingerly shifted it to a plate, dumped chips beside it, and went to the living room.

"That is enough to feed a family of eight." I made myself a turkey sandwich on whole wheat with lettuce and mayo, bypassed the chips, and sat with him on the sofa.

"I need energy for my martial arts classes. They're brutal. And so do you, for your runs. What you call a sandwich wouldn't nourish a small child. You need to eat more."

"I don't have much appetite," I said.

"Why not?"

"You know why."

"I think I do. Would it help if you said it out loud?" he asked.

Unexpectedly, talons of grief pulled me apart. I tried to clamp down on my tears.

"Come here." Zac wrapped me in his arms as I got myself together.

"It's just…I miss Aunt Ceci so much."

"I know, baby." His stomach rumbled.

"I'll let you finish your lunch," I said, drying my eyes. "Don't want you fainting from starvation."

As he ate, his phone jittered on the dining table. Suddenly, it was in my hand. I gave it to Zac.

"Hi, Dad," he answered, then listened. "What?" he shouted. "You're serious? I never would have thought…Yeah, I understand…Okay…Yeah. Talk to you soon." He ended the call and looked at me.

"What happened?" I demanded. "Is Bobby okay?"

"I can't believe it."

"Can't believe what?" I wanted to scream.

"Bobby's fine. He talked to the detective at noon." Zac took my hands and pulled me to sit beside him. "Dad said he's doing well and for you to stop worrying. His doctors are pleased and gave him a good prognosis. Bobby told Detective Hanson who tried to run you down."

I braced myself.

"It wasn't your father."

"What?" I shrieked.

Zac shook his head, apparently still digesting the news. "Dad emphasized we can't tell anyone. The sheriff's department is working on the arrest warrant."

"If not Father, then who?"

"It was Elaine," Zac said.

"Elaine?" A stiff breeze could've blown me over.

"Yes. Bobby saw her clearly." He rubbed his neck. "She must've followed us to Winnser, waiting for a chance to attack you."

"I guess that explains her behavior Saturday at the wedding. I wonder if Mrs. Van Horne knew what she'd done."

"Good question," he said. We sat with blank stares. "I never would've believed her capable. It goes to show you can never tell what people will do."

My mind chased after his statement, finally catching up. At last, I said, "Did you know she put a dead cat in my locker at the end of junior year? Elaine has always hated me, but trying to kill me…"

"A dead cat? Jesus!" He looked angry. "I'm sorry I didn't see this coming. Damn it! If I'd made it clear I wasn't getting back together with her, I might've prevented this."

"It wouldn't have made a difference. A smart person once told me we can't be responsible for other people's actions," I reminded him.

"I guess you really do listen to me."

"Yes, I do. And so should you."

Chapter Six

...Angeline and I face each other, sitting on the bed in my old room.

"I'm having a hard time believing Elaine tried to kill me," I say. "I never realized her hatred ran so deep."

"She always hated both of us," Angeline answers. "Because of Daddy."

I can't figure out what she means. "What did he do to make Elaine hate us?"

"Daddy was always finding sticky situations people wanted to keep secret. Then they would have to do things for him so he wouldn't tell," Angeline says.

"Elaine has hated us her whole life. She didn't have secrets when she was a baby."

"Not Elaine. Daddy found out about Mrs. Van Horne." At my surprised look, Angeline adds, "Mr. Van Horne wasn't Elaine's real dad. That's why they got divorced before Elaine was two."

"Father told you that?"

"Yeah. To cover it up, Mrs. Van Horne acts like she's perfect. Daddy thought it was funny to make her mad. He was always saying mean things to her."

"Wow." I trace my finger over the bedspread. "That explains a lot. No wonder Mrs. Van Horne detests us. I guess she encouraged Elaine to hate us too. Though it wasn't like we could make Father stop. We

didn't even know."

"They always thought we both knew. I felt sorry for them. If Daddy wasn't hateful, they wouldn't have turned into nasty people."

"I think they were already bad people," I say, staring at the dark window. "He just pushed them over the edge..."

****

Tuesday, September 22

The new day was beautiful. The sky was clear, the sun bright, and a cool breeze kept the temperature low. It was great for a walk. After stretching, I set out at a slow pace. I was careful to keep my gait smooth so I wouldn't aggravate my headache.

I'd spent yesterday trying to digest the fact my father wasn't really after me. I was so sure it was him, it was hard to let go of the idea.

Sheriff Rey had come by late last evening. He'd explained Elaine had been arrested and jailed. When she refused to answer questions without an attorney, he'd left the police station. Mrs. Van Horne was in the lobby, talking on her phone. She'd wanted a lawyer to come immediately to defend her "poor daughter against these outrageous allegations." With a sly grin, Sheriff Rey had added that Jayce Phelps from the *Clantonville News* pulled into the parking lot as he was leaving.

"That was fast. I wonder how he found out," I'd said.

Sheriff Rey winked at me. "Well, he may have gotten an anonymous tip."

I'd been too surprised to respond.

Zac had busted up and slapped his dad on the back. "Serves them right for being horrible to Maddie all these years."

Too perplexed to fall asleep right away, I'd ended up resting well. Zac had already left for work when I woke up with a ton of energy. Striding along, I couldn't help myself and began to trot. A weed whacker rumbled in the distance. I returned Mrs. Bennett's wave as she drove to Dorothy's Diner for her nine o'clock pastry. She hadn't missed a day in thirty years and was so punctual, clocks could be set by the ritual. A few blocks on, a dog barked behind the fence of a yard. Birds chirped in the trees. A bee missile targeted my nose. I dodged the tiny aviator and laughed.

God, what bliss! I kept my stride loose and breathed in rhythm to my steps. The air was fresh and the humidity low. I hadn't realized how heavy the burden had been, believing my own father was out there hunting me down. Relief made me lighter. It was wonderful to be alive, with my would-be killer behind bars. I picked up my pace and started to jog, my feet barely touching the ground.

An intense burn sliced the front of my thigh. Another bee? The pain was too great to be a sting. I glanced down to see an angry, red welt streaking my leg.

Shump! Fragments of bark peppered my calf.

Without thinking, I skidded to a stop and ducked behind the next tree. Another *shump* sent a vibration through the trunk.

Shit! Shit! Shit!

That was a bullet.

****

My heart tried to break out of its cage as I hid. Minutes passed without gunfire. When a car lumbered down the street, I peeked out. No shots answered, and I checked my surroundings. I didn't see feet under bushes or a head peering around a house. No glint of sun off a metal barrel.

When another car came along, I launched into a sprint, using the vehicle as a shield. When it pulled ahead, I cut from the sidewalk into the front yards. My footing wasn't as sure in the grass, but the trees between me and the street provided some cover. I figured a sprained ankle was better than a bullet hole.

Reaching Zac's house, I blew through the front door, slammed it, and twisted the deadbolt. The peephole made a dent in the back of my head as I collapsed against it, wheezing. Out of immediate danger, my legs began to wobble. I slid to the floor and sat with my head on my knees. I tried to slow my breathing to make my heart decelerate. It didn't work, and I got lightheaded. I crawled onto the sofa and pressed my cheek to the cool leather. *Get up! Call the police.* Unable to control my trembling, I couldn't have dialed the phone. Besides, the sheriff's department wouldn't be much help. They didn't have enough personnel to stage a manhunt. And who would they look for? I hadn't seen who fired at me.

But I was convinced I knew. Elaine was in jail. There was only one other person who wanted me dead, and that was my father.

****

When Angeline and I were children, Father's periodic rage created constant turmoil in our lives. I tried to hide from it. Angeline, usually not the target of his venom, distracted him by being agreeable.

When we were eight or nine years old, he'd gotten

us a puppy. It was a registered purebred. Something reflecting his taste, even a dog, had to be the best. I'd been more excited than Angeline about getting a pet, though it was her begging that had persuaded him.

I'd fallen in love with the eight-week-old cocker spaniel at first sight. He was tiny, looking forlorn with a wrinkled brow above liquid chestnut eyes. Deciding Arthur was a good name for such a lonely soul, I promised I'd take good care of him and play with him every day. He agreed to the bargain by licking my chin. I cuddled him until Father made me come inside and go to bed. In the middle of the night, he was still whining on the deck, and I'd crept out to sit with him. He crawled onto my lap and fell asleep. I sucked in a breath. It was the first time I'd felt needed.

The next afternoon, I'd run from the school bus to search for Arthur. He wasn't on the deck. I looked underneath it, in the back yard, and by the wading pond with growing alarm. I couldn't find him anywhere. Tearing inside, I asked Mother where he was.

"The dog was too stupid to stay out of the road. He got run over," she said.

"No!" I wailed.

"See for yourself if you don't believe me. He landed in the ditch."

I turned from her and bolted. I found Arthur lying in the grass. He looked even smaller, like a half-inflated ball. His body wasn't warm like the night before. I placed him on my knees and petted him as I cried. I'd promised to take care of him, and I'd let him die.

Before long, Angeline came to get me. I was inconsolable and refused to go in with her. When Father came home, he didn't notice me slumped on the lawn.

The front door slammed when he came out for me. He yanked me from the ground by the arm. "You stupid idiot. Begging me for a dog that gets killed as soon as I've paid for it." He lowered his face to mine, yelling, "Shut up!" He shook me, making my head whip back and forth. I tried to stop crying, but I was too scared.

Angeline surged out of the house. "Daddy, Daddy! Don't you want to see my math test?" She squeezed between us, laying her hands on his cheeks. "I got an 'A' just like you said I would. It was easy after you helped me last night. Come look at it."

He straightened, smoothing his hair to gather his composure. "Okay, honey," he said calmly to Angeline.

She clasped his hand and pulled him toward the house.

He took a couple of steps then spun to me. "I don't want that to stink. Get rid of it. Then go to bed."

I carried Arthur to a place by the pond, then got a shovel out of the tool garage. Sobbing, I dug a hole as best I could, then gently covered him with dirt.

Late that night, Angeline snuck into my room. "I'm sorry Arthur's gone. Try not to cry." She wrapped her arms around me.

"Thanks for making Father stop shaking me," I'd said, wiping my nose.

"I should've gotten there sooner. I will next time. Promise," Angeline had whispered.

The memory left me hollow as I lay on the couch letting the adrenaline rush wear off. It was one of the countless times Angeline had protected me. How much had she endured to shield me from him? As a child, I'd been oblivious to his abuse, how he'd made her life a nightmare. I should've been the one protecting her. I rubbed the goosebumps on my arm.

God damn him! Fury swelled inside, searing my stomach, shattering the box I'd locked it in. I'd promised to make my father pay for the hell he'd put Angeline through. I clenched my fists, getting up to pace. I should have acted weeks ago to track him down. I wouldn't let him get away without punishment.

My anger coalesced into a plan. Immediately, I put it in motion with a phone call.

Jayce Phelps sounded surprised when I said I'd like more information put in tomorrow's paper. He was kind, agreeing to add a few lines to the paragraph reporting my hospital stay.

With the first task out of the way, I saw it was later than I'd thought. Step two of my strategy was crucial, and I had to drive beyond the reach of Clantonville's gossips to do it.

I called Mrs. Wells. She answered in a high falsetto.

"Hi, there. This is Madisen Chandler," I said. "Thank you for sending the flowers. They were beautiful."

"Why, Maddie, what a surprise! I'm glad you liked them."

"How are you?"

"I'm fine, child. My joints are better today." At eighty-six, she suffered from arthritis and couldn't get around well. She spent most of her time on the phone relaying gossip: everything from who had dinner with whom to the latest bingo winners.

Though I had a healthy dislike of people who spread hearsay, I couldn't seem to hold it against her.

"That's good to hear." Before she launched into a

discourse regarding who needed a get-well card for their hemorrhoid surgery, I asked to borrow her car.

"Well, I suppose that'd be all right. It's a little temperamental, but it's never left me stranded."

"Thank you so much. I'll be there in a few minutes." Before she had a chance to get a word in, I said, "Goodbye now," and hung up.

Still in my running clothes, I locked up and got going before I could rethink my decision. I didn't enjoy the exercise as I had earlier that morning, too worried I could be shot. I told myself Father wouldn't expect me out again so soon and kept running.

The mile to Mrs. Wells's house went quickly at my frantic pace. Puffing as much from anxiety as exertion, I took the porch steps two at a time. She lived in an older neighborhood, next door to the house Aunt Ceci had given me.

"Land sakes!" she said when she'd hobbled to the door. "I would've come pick you up. I didn't know you'd have to run all the way over here with a concussion and all."

"Oh, you didn't need to go to the trouble," I said, catching my breath. "My head's fine."

"Come in and sit a spell. We can catch up on the news."

"I'm sorry, I don't have time to chat or do dishes today. I'm in a bit of a hurry and need to get going."

"It's sweet of you to think of me, but I don't expect you to clean every time you come over. I'm fixin' to hire someone. Just haven't gotten around to finding the right person. Let me get the keys," she said, shuffling to her bedroom.

"I appreciate the use of your car," I said again

when she returned.

"To get it to start, you have to pump the gas one time, then hit the ignition for only a second. Then it'll start right away. It runs a little rough till it warms up."

"Okay. I'll be careful."

I drove the twelve-year-old sedan to Zac's house and jumped in the shower. In too much of a rush to find a fresh outfit, I threw on my jeans from a couple of days ago, slipped into a T-shirt, grabbed my purse, and darted out with wet hair.

Heading west on State Highway 7 through rolling pastures and fields, I reached Harrelson in forty-five minutes. For most of the drive, I kept one eye on the mirror to see if I was being followed.

I was fortunate a highway patrol didn't spot me. I was driving well over the speed limit. Once in town, I parked at a pharmacy to look up directions to the gun store. Ten minutes later, I pulled in front of the building. The urge to run inside was strong, but I made myself walk.

Sporting Supplies had been in business longer than I could remember, though I'd never been inside. Deer heads hung on the wall, and a full-body-mount taxidermy coyote posed atop a shelf. Two men were at the long counter, and a salesman helped a third in the bow-hunting section. I hoped the male staff wouldn't ignore me. It didn't look like many women frequented the place.

One of the customers turned to leave as I walked to the counter. He looked startled, then broke into a broad grin, nodding a polite hello. The employee beamed at me. My worry about not getting help was put to rest. It seemed the opposite. They were happy to see a female.

"Hello," I said. "My name is Maddie. I'd like to buy a handgun."

"Nice to meet you, Maddie. I'm Walt. We've got a big selection to choose from." He was a slender man in his fifties, with a shellacked comb-over and bushy brows. He wore a plaid flannel shirt. "What type are you looking for?"

I went blank. "Uh, I don't know anything about guns." I peeked at him under my lashes. "What would you recommend?"

Walt leaned forward like a co-conspirator. "If you're not experienced with firearms, I'd recommend a revolver. They won't jam and are simple to load and unload. It's easy to tell how many shots are left, and you won't have to worry about a clip." He pulled three from the display case. "This is a snub-nose thirty-eight special. These two are nine-millimeter."

He handed me a nine-millimeter. "It's not loaded, right?" I asked before accepting it. Walt shook his head. I held the gun up, looking along the sight. "It weighs more than I thought it would."

"It's steel. We have some polymer models. Since they're lighter, they tend to have more muzzle rise when fired and are harder to control."

"He's right, a revolver is best," another customer said. "Didn't mean to eavesdrop," he added when I glanced his way. He wore dirty jeans and had a week's worth of stubble. "And you don't want polymer. Go with the steel."

I nodded, shifting my attention back to the guns. The thirty-eight special wasn't as heavy, and the grip fit my hand better. "So, what happens when you run out of bullets?"

"You press this lever to release the cylinder, then remove the casings and put new ones in."

"Reloading isn't very fast. I guess I'll have to get the job done with five shots."

"That'd be right," Walt agreed. "You can fire using only the trigger, or you can pull the hammer back first. That way the trigger has less resistance."

Imitating a gunslinger, I cupped my right hand over the top and pulled back the hammer. When I released it, the skin between my thumb and finger was pinched hard. *Ouch! That hurt!*

Walt tried to hide his smirk.

"Can I shoot the thirty-eight special and a nine-millimeter?"

"Of course. If you're sure you'll buy today, you can go ahead and fill out the Department of Justice form," Walt said. "I'll run the history check while you're at the range."

"I'm definitely buying today," I said.

He retrieved papers from a drawer under the display. I filled them out quickly, pausing only at the question asking if I'd ever been adjudicated mentally defective.

Not yet.

I checked "no" and added my signature.

Chapter Seven

Walt looked over the paperwork. "You live in Texas?" he asked.

The furrow of his brow made me wary. Was this an issue? I came up with an indirect answer that wasn't an outright lie. "It's the address on my driver's license."

"Oh." He seemed relieved. "If you haven't gotten a Missouri license yet, you'll have to give some kind of confirmation you reside in the state."

"I own a home in Henry County." Again, not technically a lie.

Walt thought a moment and said, "If the utilities are in your name, a bill would work."

"I happen to have some right here." I pulled the envelopes from my pocket that Carlos had given me two days before.

Walt passed me a new form. I put down Aunt Ceci's address on the "residence" line, filled out the rest, and handed it back along with the bills and my driver's license. Walt compared the two forms, confirming the address was the only change, then waved over a young man who rested his elbows on the glass.

"Toby here will take you back," he said.

Picking up the handguns, Toby led me down a hall to the rear of the building. In a small lobby, I put my name on a clipboard as he pulled out ammunition and ear protection.

The firing range's floor, ceiling, and walls were concrete. It looked like a bunker. Shell casings were scattered beyond the booths. No one else was there. At least Toby would be the only witness to my first attempt at firing a gun.

He placed the thirty-eight special and three bullets on the small counter and moved the cardboard target about ten feet away. Then he stepped behind me and put on the earmuffs. I put mine on too and loaded the gun.

I carefully lined up the sight to dead center, took a breath, and exhaled as I pulled the trigger. *My God, that was loud.* The gun jumped in my hand more than I'd expected. There was a bullet hole in the cardboard three-quarters up from the bottom. At least I'd hit it.

"Can we move the target back?" I asked through the ringing in my ears.

"Sure thing." He showed me the button in the booth that adjusted the pulley mechanism.

At twenty feet, I aimed a little lower and hit the target almost on center. At thirty feet, I hit between the first and second shot. Not bad for a beginner.

With the nine-millimeter, I shot from farther away on the second and third try, which I missed. It was even louder, and the barrel rise was harder to control.

"I like the thirty-eight best," I said to Toby. He nodded, leading the way back to the store.

An hour later and seven hundred ninety dollars lighter, I left. I'd acquired a gun, fifty rounds of ammunition (100-grain hollow-point bullets), and a leather purse designed for women who carried. It had a matching leather holster with a belt loop in the side zip pocket. Also, I'd bought a maintenance kit with cleaning solution, a rod, brass bristle brush, cotton cloth, and oil.

I didn't expect to use the cleaning kit. If I had to shoot the gun, it would be to kill my father before he killed me. I hoped never to pick up a firearm again.

Inside the old four-door, I changed purses. I put the cleaning kit and ammunition in the new purse as well and zipped the holstered gun into its compartment. Then I put my old purse in the plain white shopping bag and pumped the gas once.

Driving away, I felt different. Like there was a sign on the car proclaiming I carried a weapon. I took three deep breaths and swiped my palms down my legs. I didn't want to think about the fact I had the means to choose if someone lived or died. Instead, I concentrated on the security it provided. I was determined to stand up for myself, and if that meant taking Father's life to save mine, I'd do it. "No room for doubt," I said aloud.

I clenched the wheel to steady my hands and drove to Clantonville under the speed limit.

****

Zac was home by the time Mrs. Wells dropped me off. To ease my jitters, I paused at the door before walking in.

Inside, I took in the glowing candles scattered across the coffee and dining tables. The lights were off. As my vision adjusted to the dimness, Zac walked out of the bathroom wearing only a towel. I watched a drop of water slide down his chest and get lost in the ripples of his abs. *Jesus, his body is perfect.* I bit my lip when his beautiful chocolate gaze met mine.

He stalked to me.

"Have you been wait—?" I began.

He put a finger to my mouth. "Shh." Holding my stare, he put my purse and shopping bag on the sofa.

My heart beat faster, and this time it wasn't from fear.

He lifted my top and touched his lips to the bullet scar on my hip. He inched the cloth up slowly, brushing my ribs with his knuckles.

"Raise your arms," he said. He pulled the shirt over my head and his breath caught.

I glanced down, thankful to see sexy lace instead of a sports bra.

Zac stared at my breasts beneath lowered lids. I reached to touch him, and he moved my hands to my sides.

"Don't move," he murmured. "Don't speak. This is about you. Shut your eyes to heighten your other senses. With every touch, each taste of you, when I breathe the scent of your skin, I want you to know how much you mean to me."

My eyes misted at his words. I closed them. It seemed a long time passed, my anticipation rising as I waited. I felt a caress on my head.

Zac massaged my scalp and lifted my hair. His lips touched the nape of my neck, sending ripples along my spine.

He skimmed his hands down my legs and untied my shoes. "Take them off," he said.

I slipped out of them without looking.

He unbuttoned my jeans, and I heard the zipper purr as he slid it down.

Zac nudged the fly apart, kissing along the top of my panties as he tugged the jeans down. He placed my hand on his shoulder and lifted each foot out. I stood before him in only my underthings.

"My God," he whispered. "I'll never get over how beautiful you are." My cheeks heated, and he kissed behind my ear. I tilted my head as he ran his tongue up the outside edge.

"Mmm." I sighed.

His forehead settled against mine. "Never forget I can't live without you," he said. "More than good enough, you're better than I deserve." His comments made my lids open. Sincerity and desire stared back at me.

He kissed my eyes closed and moved away, unhooking my bra and moving it down my arms. For a long moment, he didn't touch me, at last murmuring, "Baby, you're gorgeous." A fingertip stroked my collarbone, down to the swell of my breast, and up again before retracing the path. Each time the caress got closer to my aching nipple, I arched into his touch. Finally, his tongue stroked the swollen nub, making me gasp.

"Oh, Maddie." He sighed. Taking both my hands, he led me to the bedroom.

****

It was after midnight. Zac and I lay entwined after making love three times to satisfy our desire. Exhausted, I fell into a contented slumber.

...Like an embrace, the warm night air blankets my skin. The water is cool on my feet as I wade in the pond with Angeline.

"Father shot at me this morning," I say.

"Oh, no! I wanted him to stop hating you. But he's not going to, is he." It isn't a question. Angeline's

expression is miserable. "I'm sorry."

"Don't apologize. You didn't make him despise me."

She fidgets her feet, sending ripples across the surface. "It is my fault. He always knew I loved you more than him."

I take her by the hand, lead her to the grass, and pull her down beside me. Resting a palm on her shoulder, I say, "Loving your twin sister does not make what he did your fault. Father is deranged. He's a psychopath and a bastard. He abused you, and I'm going to make him pay for it."

Angeline's chin shudders. "I don't want you to get hurt, Maddie. You should leave."

"No. If I go to Texas, he'll just follow me. I won't run away, and I refuse to live in fear of him. I'm going to bring this to an end. It'll be okay, Angeline." Even as I reassure her, I know it's not true. "One way or another, it'll all be over soon."

I pull her to me and hold her as she cries...

****

Wednesday, September 23

Zac's soft kiss when he left for work barely stirred my sleep. I woke later in a serene mood, thinking of our lovemaking the night before. When he kissed me, he'd inhaled my sighs of euphoria. It touched my heart. I didn't understand how he made me feel complete. I only knew that, without him, I wasn't whole.

My tranquility faded as I recalled Angeline's tears.

As soon as I'd finished my morning routine and gotten dressed, Zac's front door slammed with such ferocity, the entire house shook.

"Maddie!" he shouted. He was *angry*.

The Art of Being Broken

I rushed into the living room. His back was turned, the *News* clutched in his fist.

"What's wrong?" I asked.

He wheeled around. "What the fuck is this?" he demanded, flinging the paper at my feet.

"What are you talking about?"

"Don't pretend you don't know! Jayce Phelps's article." He pointed at the paper. "It says you're staying at your father's house. That you're clearing it out and turning it into a rental. He won't stand for that. You might as well paint a target on your back."

"I wan—"

"Oh my God! You made that up to lure him out of hiding. Using yourself as bait!" He pressed shaking fists to his head. "Do you think so little of me?"

For the first time since he'd barged in, I noticed his eyes. They were haunted. Shimmering fountains of pain.

What? "No…It has nothing to do with you. I—"

"How can you say that? It has everything to do with me. Why didn't we discuss this? Do I figure in your life at all?"

"Of course you do." My lungs failed. I couldn't find a way to explain. "It's just…"

"You just didn't consider my feelings? Or how this could affect my future?" he implored.

I could only stare, dumbfounded.

"Did you bother to take the family into account? The people who love you? Did you think what it would do to us if you got hurt again? If you were killed, Maddie, how could I go on? After last night, I thought…"

He stabbed me with a look so distraught, I

instinctively reached for him. He reeled away like a wounded animal. A tear dribbled down his cheek.

Oh, Christ! He was right. I'd acted without considering anyone else. I swallowed thickly. "I thought—"

"No, you didn't think!" He turned away. "You know what? I can't do this."

Glued in place, I watched as he strode out the door. With a snick, it closed behind him. Cold inched from my toes into my legs and torso. It froze my heart, making it shatter. I don't know how long I stood there, unconnected to reality and untouched by time.

****

I found myself on the floor in the bathroom with no memory of how I got there. I'd been sick in the toilet. A sob escaped as I dragged myself up and turned on the light. At the sink, I rubbed absently at a twinge on my cheek. The person in the mirror copied the movement, but I didn't recognize her. My fingers came away wet.

In the bedroom, I hurled things into my suitcase. Like an out-of-body experience, I saw myself gathering my clothes, leaving whatever spilled from my arms where it fell.

What have you done, Madisen? What have you done?

****

My phone beeped with Tabs's reply to the text I'd sent.

—Of course, you can use the car, hon. I'm in a meeting. Keys in visor. Later.—

Relieved I wouldn't have to answer her questions about what had upset me, I threw the phone into my open suitcase and tied my running shoes.

Tabs worked at a discount store over two miles from Zac's house. I took off at an all-out sprint. It was useless, though. I'd never be able to outrun myself.

The punishing pace soon made my lungs burn, and the struggle to breathe put an end to my sobs. It helped to have physical pain to distract from my emotional torment.

I suddenly envied Aunt Ceci. The dead were beyond sorrow's reach.

Once I got to the small sedan, I gasped as if I'd nearly drowned. Lack of oxygen caused dark blots in my vision. I rested in the car until my surroundings stopped whirling. The tires squealed when I sped from the parking lot. At Zac's, I closed my suitcase, grabbed my bags, heaved them into the trunk, and drove away.

Having blown my life apart, I fled the destruction.

No other cars were in sight on the rural highway. I pulled onto a gravel side road and let go. Primal moans and guttural sobs erupted from me. I collapsed on the steering wheel, barely summoning the strength to wipe my streaming eyes. Wailing and retching, I gave in to the unbearable loss and wept until congestion made it impossible to breathe.

I'd let Zac in. Taken down my walls and trusted him with my heart, assuming he would always forgive my selfishness. Then I'd carelessly mauled his feelings. No wonder he'd had enough. I'd sacrificed the future by alienating the most important person in my life. Regret emptied me, savage in its boiling rush. If only I could rewind, go back in time and regain his affection.

It's too late. He's gone.

Exhaustion eventually quieted my groans, though not my tears. They continued to slink down my cheeks.

The salt left my skin dehydrated. I steered the car northwest toward Kansas City without aim or purpose. At the interstate, I pulled into a gas station. People went about their business, oblivious, as I got out to fill the tank. I was baffled. Couldn't they see the world was in ruins? I slammed the door against their apathy.

The University Medical Health Center. Yes, I'd go there. Talking to Bobby might reassure me I hadn't ruined his life as I had mine. I found it on the car's GPS and set the route.

Chapter Eight

"Swee'ness, I think you look worse than I do." Bobby's words were a little slurred. "Wha's wrong?"

The room was only large enough to fit the bed, two chairs, and a nightstand. The monitoring equipment blinked in the dim light. For an hour, I'd curled up in a chair as he slept. I'd managed to keep the occasional sob quiet by biting my lip. *Maybe you shouldn't have come.* Once the decision was made, though, the car had steered itself as I rode along in a zombie-like haze.

"How are you feeling?" I asked, hiding my sadness as I stood.

He gave me a silly grin. "Like I got hit by a car," he quipped. Despite his mischievous tone, he was pale and had a bad case of bedhead. He didn't wear a gown, revealing the bandages that covered the lower half of his rib cage and continued beneath the covers at his waist. Ugly red and black bruises stained the left half of his exposed chest.

His comment made fresh tears flow. "No…Hey," he said. "Don't cry. After some therapy for my leg, I'll be good as new. Come 'ere." He reached with his right arm and tugged me close, encircling my waist. "Lie down with me."

"No, I can't. I—" I almost said I had a boyfriend. Not anymore. "I'll hurt you."

"It won't hurt, swee'ness. They give me great pain

meds. I can't feel a thing. Come on." I hesitantly sat on the edge of the bed. "Put your head on my shoulder."

What the hell. It's not like you'd be cheating. I stretched out, careful to touch him only with my temple. He pulled me tight against him, letting out a sigh. "Yeah, this is nice."

I finally relaxed when Bobby had fallen asleep.

"Now, why are you upset?"

He wasn't sleeping after all.

"I've destroyed my life."

"I'm sure it's not that bad. Tell me what happened." When I stayed quiet, he said, "In my 'sperience, there's only one cause for a woman being this upset. And that's a man. Is it on account of your boyfriend?"

"He left me."

"He's an asshole," Bobby said. I stiffened. "Sorry, but he is. If I was him, I'd never let you go."

"I'm selfish and inconsiderate." My voice trembled. "I don't deserve him. Zac's better off without me."

"I don't believe it. Unless he's an idiot, he'll come back. Trust me on that."

I shook my head, suppressing a sob.

"Okay, what'd you do that was so selfish?" he asked.

"I made a life-changing decision without discussing it with him."

"Will he be affected by it?"

"He could be, yes."

"Hmm. Can you change your mind?"

"No," I said. "Even if I could undo it, I wouldn't. It's a promise I made. I have to see it through."

"I guess the only choice you have is to say 'sorry' and explain why it's important. He should support your decision if it means that much to you."

"It's not that simple."

"How come?"

"I might get hurt. Even killed."

"What?" Bobby blurted. "You serious?"

I nodded against his shoulder.

"I don't know what to say. Guess if I was him, I'd lock you up to keep you from doing something stupid."

I didn't answer.

"You gonna tell me what it is?"

"No."

"You owe me one since I saved your life," he said, only half teasing.

"I know I do. Thank you. I'll never be able to repay you."

"Well, if you won't tell me, promise you'll reconsider."

"I can't."

"Okay, promise me you won't get hurt."

"Can't do that, either."

"Will you promise to try?"

I lifted my head and looked into his eyes. "Yes."

I felt better for having confided in someone. I rested my head on Bobby's shoulder again. Soon, his soft snores told me he was asleep this time. I took advantage of his willingness to hold me. God knew Zac never would again.

A nurse came in. I pretended to sleep. She stood for a while, probably debating whether to kick me out. Then she made an adjustment to Bobby's monitoring equipment and left. Grateful, I stayed, secure in

Bobby's warmth.

Eventually, I detached myself and slipped off the bed without waking him. I tiptoed to the door. Opening it, I found Amber in the hall about to reach for the knob. Tony was with her.

"Oh, hi," I said, joining them.

"Hi, Madisen," Tony piped up. "We're going to see my daddy!"

"He's napping right now. I'm sure he'll be happy you're here." I noticed Amber's limp hair and the dark circles under her eyes. "I'm sorry," I choked out.

She gave me a hug, also unable to speak.

"You don't gotta be sorry," Tony said, throwing his arms around both of us. "You weren't driving the car that ran him over. Auntie Elaine was. Well, she's not really my aunt. That's just what she wants me to call her."

"Tony, shh," Amber told him.

"Your dad wouldn't have gotten hurt if I hadn't been there," I said, squatting to his level. "So, it is my fault."

"Nuh-uh. You didn't do nothing wrong."

"Your dad's a hero," I said around the lump in my throat. "You know that, right?"

"Like Superman?"

"He's better. He ran faster than the car and pushed me out of the way. He saved me. Even Superman couldn't have done that."

"Cool!" he said.

I straightened to see Amber nodding. "You're not to blame," she said.

"Thank you," I answered, cherishing their gift of forgiveness.

In the parking garage, I looked for my phone, then remembered it was in my suitcase. I used the car's GPS again to find a hotel near the airport. There were at least a dozen. I picked one at random since I wouldn't be staying in it.

The conversation with Bobby had helped clear my head. I'd also had the chance to rework my original plan and was more determined than ever. If the price I had to pay was living without Zac, by God I was going to finish this with Father.

Yesterday, I was focused on defending my decisions during our confrontation and hadn't considered Zac's reaction. I knew Sheriff Rey's response would be the same: fury that I was putting myself in danger. They'd do anything to stop me. But the breakup with Zac gave me a way to keep them out of danger. I could concentrate on my own survival.

That's ironic. Without Zac you don't have much to live for.

The grass along Interstate 35 grew thick and tall from the recent rains. Traffic was light in the early afternoon. I made good time north on Route 169 and followed the GPS as it directed me onto Interstate 29. Candletree Hotel and Suites was easy to find.

Thankfully, the front entrance had automatic doors. Though Zac could lift my heavy bag easily, heaving it over the threshold made me stagger. The clerk at the front desk had a Santa Claus face minus the beard. He had dark hair, a round tummy, and an Indian accent.

We exchanged pleasantries. I requested a room at the end of a hall, close to stairs with an exterior exit. It would explain why I wasn't seen coming and going through the lobby. When asked, I said I'd need the room until Sunday and handed him my credit card. He processed my payment as he studied me. I knew my skin was blotchy and that I must look terrible.

"Are you all right, miss?"

"Yes," I said. "I've been at the hospital. A friend of mine was injured in an accident. He's going to make it. I'll stay a few more days then book a flight home. I just need some rest."

"Oh," he replied with a sympathetic nod. "I'm glad to hear your friend will be okay."

****

Neat and clean, the room had two queen beds and walls painted a peaceful shade of blue. After a quick shower, I hauled the suitcase atop the table. Digging through the tangle, I found a clean pair of yoga pants, running bra, and shirt. I rolled up a pair of shorts, two shirts, socks, some panties, and stuffed them in my old purse, along with my toothbrush, toothpaste, and phone charger. Then I pulled the bedding down and rumpled a pillow.

The plan to keep my friends safe when I confronted my father included sending two messages to Tabs. I hoped to mislead her, and everyone she might tell, about my location. I typed the first one:

—Thanks again for letting me use your car. It'll be there when you finish work. I'm going to visit Bobby with his sister, Amber. Back too late tonight to call. We'll catch up tomorrow.—

Finished, I hit send and turned off my phone in case it was traced, then grabbed the purses. To get Tabs's car back before five o'clock, I'd have to hurry. I galloped down the stairs and out the door, wishing I could leave my problems behind along with my luggage.

****

The employee parking area at Tabs's work had one empty space. Once there, I crisscrossed the long purse straps over my chest and managed to leave the car without being noticed. Keeping close to the building, I walked to the back. The discount store was on the edge of town and abutted open pasture. I could cut across the countryside to my father's house and stay out of sight.

Feeling small under the vast sky, I slipped between two strands of barbed wire, careful not to snag my clothes. In mid-September, central west Missouri was a quilt of soybean and corn fields, some still awaiting harvest. Lines of fence divided the pastures. Trees and brush grew along the creeks. Occasionally, hay bales as large as I was tall dotted the meadows, and ponds provided water for cattle.

As I scurried over the rough clumps of grass in the pasture, fresh memories of Zac swamped me. Even more than I longed to see Aunt Ceci, I ached to get a glimpse of him. To watch as his eyes crinkled when he smiled. I wanted to be cocooned in his solid dependability when we hugged. At least with the breakup, I'd never have to tell him I had conversations with my dead sister. The thought wasn't much comfort.

After crawling through another fence, my attention strayed, and I stepped in a fresh cow pile. Damn! I wiped most of it off in the grass, hoping the smell wouldn't give me away inside Father's house. Half a mile later, I found a place in the grass under some trees where I could wait for sunset. Careful to avoid manure this time, I sat quietly and rested.

Against my closed lids, a memory played in the

theater of my mind.

After the final bell, junior high was deserted except for me, Macy Harvey, LeeAnne Dickson, and Elaine van Horne. I stared into my locker, trying to ignore their whispers. Elaine deliberately spoke so I could hear.

"Angeline was the pretty one. I think Maddie's happy her sister's dead. She was jealous."

I'd snatched up my backpack and slammed the metal door. The echoing crash covered the sound of Zac walking up behind the girls.

"There you are, Maddie," he said. "I'll give you a ride."

The other three goggled when they saw the best-looking guy in high school take my bag. Their mouths were still open when he put an arm around my shoulder as we walked. This time, their whispers were too low to hear.

"I wish you'd let me put them in their place," Zac said when we were outside. "I hate that they're mean to you."

"Thanks for offering, but I can fight my own battles. Besides, it wouldn't shut them up for long, and they'd just hate me more. Macy's dad had an appointment with my father the other day. Mr. Harvey must be in big trouble if he's hiring Father for criminal defense. She assumes I know what's going on."

"Then fight fire with fire. Tell them to leave you alone, or you'll make sure everyone hears about it."

"Nah," I answered. "Making them miserable won't stop them."

From the driver's seat of his six-year-old clunker, he gave me a penetrating look. "You're a better person than all of them put together." He pushed my hair behind my ear, and I felt his breath on my cheek before he kissed it. His scent of fresh hay almost made me hyperventilate, and my heartbeat doubled. "And they lied when they said you aren't pretty." He started the car, and I wished I could hide the pink infusing my skin.

The memory faded. Before I rose to brush off the dust, I took the gun and box of bullets from my purse. The day before, I'd had mixed emotions about the weapon. But with every passing hour, I came to see it as my only means of self-protection. I loaded it, stuck it in my waistband, and walked on.

****

The sun had vanished, and the half-moon hung low in the eastern sky. I was lying twenty yards from the back deck, hidden behind the blackberry bushes by the fence. Greasy anxiety roiled my stomach. Though there was no sign my father was inside, surely Sheriff Rey or Detective Hanson would be watching the house.

An hour after sundown, the darkness was complete. I crept on hands and knees along the fence toward the center of the three acres. In this section of the long, rectangular lot, trees between the house and pond would provide cover.

When clouds drifted across the moon, I crawled beneath the fence and made my way through the undergrowth. I stopped when I had a clear view of the front yard and road. Crouched amid the foliage, I saw nothing. No car sat in the drive. No one seemed to be around. I waited patiently, even though I hadn't eaten all day and was getting shaky. Soon, a patrol car moved slowly past. I stayed put until another deputy's car went by an hour later. The frequent drive-bys meant the sheriff's department couldn't spare the manpower for a stakeout.

Retracing my path, I snuck to my original position behind the house. I didn't want to think about what would happen if my father was already there. Nothing in the yard was large enough to hide behind. At a gap in the bushes, I braced my left hand on a post, vaulted over the fence, and sprinted to the double doors of the lawnmower garage in the basement. To my immense relief, they weren't locked.

Bad memories fouled the atmosphere indoors like stale cigarettes. In the dark, I pulled the gun from my waistband and felt my way through the storage area. The door's creak was loud when I pushed it open to the empty playroom. My head felt thick with dread as I listened for a response to the noise. When none came, I climbed upstairs to the main floor without a sound.

Even without lights, I could see a layer of dust had settled in the weeks since Father had been away. Everything was the same as when I'd left ten years ago. No, that wasn't right. Nothing had changed since Angeline died. The living room was immaculate, its classic design impeccable. The ornate furnishings were uninviting. There were no personal touches: no photos or children's art, no knickknacks. Nothing of sentimental value. My father hated clutter and always demanded such "junk" be thrown away. The decor was a façade masking the cruelty living inside, just like Father's perfectly tailored suits.

On the ground floor and upstairs, I checked each room and closet using the flashlight on my phone, every place a person could hide. When I'd confirmed I was alone in the house, I went back to the spacious kitchen and felt around the dim pantry. Though I was hungry, I had little appetite. Knowing I needed to eat, I grabbed the first can I came to. It was beef stew. Without thinking, I put it in the electric can opener. The noise, amplified in the dead quiet, made me jump.

Yes! The utilities were on. Father's accountant handled both personal and business expenses. She must have continued paying the bills. That meant I could access the Internet, cutting down on the use of my phone and the chances my location would be pinpointed.

The *Clantonville News* was published once a week. In addition, the articles were posted on their website along with daily updates first thing in the morning. I could check it for sightings of my father.

I grabbed a spoon and ate the gloppy beef and vegetables straight from the can without tasting it. Rinsing both when I was done, I threw the can in the trash and replaced the spoon in the drawer. There was one thing I needed to do before I used the computer.

It was time to send Tabs my second text. I grabbed my phone and turned it on. It immediately chimed the notification for new messages.

Chapter Nine

Before I typed the message to Tabs, I noticed one from Zac asking where I was. We weren't together anymore. I didn't see a reason I should answer. I deleted the dozen messages he'd sent without reading them, remembering his whisper, "You're my life, baby. My whole world."

Telling myself I'd cried enough over losing him, I pushed him from my mind. I'd fooled myself into believing that with him, I'd learned to make love. Since I hadn't been able to put his needs before mine, it turned out I was only having sex.

Tabs had also texted, asking where I was and why Zac was looking for me. Using that as my opening, I wrote —*Zac broke up with me! I can't bring myself to stay in Clantonville one second longer. Bobby's half sister Amber dropped me off at a hotel close to the airport. Not ready to talk about it yet. I'll let you know when I book a flight.*—

I was sure she'd pass the information along to Zac who would tell Sheriff Rey. If they believed I was out of town, they'd also think I'd given up my plan to lure Father into a confrontation. Tabs would be hurt I hadn't confided in her. I felt awful about the deception. I told myself I would apologize—to her and everyone else I'd lied to—when it was over. At this point, keeping the people I loved out of harm's way was more important

The Art of Being Broken

than honesty.

And if I didn't live to tell them I was sorry? I couldn't face the thought.

I turned off the phone again and found my way along the hall to the office. At the desk, I flicked on the computer. Coming to life, the screen flashed in the murky room. I rushed to the window to yank the curtains shut.

A picture of Angeline sat by the keyboard. She was pretty in a new dress that matched the blue of her eyes. I ran my finger along a crack in the glass, probably from one of Father's fits of rage. To this day, I was unsure why his grief had shifted to blaming me for her death. I only knew the resentment had bloomed into hatred. I set the picture down.

Back on task, I pulled up the newspaper's website. The headline for the latest update was huge:

CLANTONVILLE WOMAN ARRESTED ON SUSPICION OF ATTEMPTED MURDER

Elaine van Horne of Clantonville was arrested by Henry County Sheriff Leland Irvine and his deputies in the late afternoon on Monday. Ms. Van Horne was charged with attempted murder with a vehicle for an incident Friday evening in Winnser, Missouri.

The probable-cause affidavit, filed by Detective John M. Hanson of the county sheriff's department, states Van Horne is suspected of striking Robert William "Bobby" Wittford with her vehicle on Houston Street.

At 7:30 p.m., the sheriff's department

dispatcher received a call reporting the incident. Mr. Wittford, a resident of Winnser for nine years, was taken via life flight to the University Medical Health Center. He underwent surgery Friday night for internal bleeding and an open fracture of the femur which broke into three pieces. Monday morning, Detective Hanson interviewed Wittford in the hospital. Without hesitation, he positively identified Ms. Van Horne as the driver of the vehicle that struck him.

Within six hours of Wittford's statement, prosecuting attorney Powell Hughes obtained an arrest warrant from Henry County Judge William LeFay. Officers found Ms. Van Horne at the residence she shares with her mother, Mrs. Caroline van Horne. Elaine van Horne was taken into custody without incident and booked into Henry County Jail. She had not been released at the time of this post.

Thankfully, no connection was made between Bobby's injury and my overnight stay in the hospital. I shook my head. I still couldn't get over the level of animosity Elaine felt toward me. Well, Zac was free, and she could have him. The realization made my throat prickle. I bit my cheek until it passed.

The short story resulting from my interviews with Phelps was posted as well. I read the summary of my hospital stay and my intent to prepare Father's house as a rental by donating its contents to charity.

I'd refused to answer Phelps's questions about the shooting in July and hadn't speculated where my father might be hiding. He hadn't added his own theories. He'd probably exhausted the topic in previous stories.

So far, all the pieces of my plan were falling into place. The last one hinged on my father reading the local news. It was the easiest way for him to find out if I was in town. I was gambling on him checking it since he wouldn't want to miss a chance to punish me.

A new item grabbed my attention when it popped up on the screen. An emergency alert, with a short news blurb attached, read:

> Lee's Summit, MO AMBER Alert:
> LIC/998FEJ (MO) 2012 Tan Ford Taurus
> Alert type: AMBER Alert
> Severity: SEVERE—Significant threat to life or property
> Urgency: Immediate—Significant action should be taken immediately
> Alert response type: Other events
> Certainty: Observed—Determined to have occurred or to be ongoing
>
> Grace Sloan, 5, was missing today when her mother, Lauren Sloan, arrived to pick her up from Persimmon Hill Elementary in Lee's Summit. She was last seen on the playground holding the hand of an older man described by witnesses as slender, approximately five feet ten inches tall, having short gray hair, and wearing dark slacks and a white button shirt.
>
> Lauren Sloan is the daughter of Deborah Redondo, 57, former spouse of Corporal Reynard (Sheriff Rey) Redondo of the Henry County Sheriff's Department and a resident of

Clantonville. The three attended the burial service of Cecilia Ortiz on July 2nd of this year.

My agonized scream punctured the tomb-like silence. No. God, please! Not an innocent five-year-old.

This couldn't be happening.

It had to be Father who took Grace. The description matched him. It couldn't be a coincidence she disappeared the same day I'd sent him a clear challenge.

She'd done nothing to deserve the attention of that monster. I pounded my fists on the desk. Fury possessed me, the same blinding rage as when I'd learned my father had been abusing Angeline. I would've physically attacked him then if I hadn't been restrained. I'd made my feelings clear about harming children. He would've known I'd go out of my mind when he abducted Grace, fearing he might abuse her like he had Angeline.

I'd underestimated him. He'd answered my ultimatum by taking advantage of a weakness I'd overlooked, despite my efforts to protect the people close to me. As a result, Grace would suffer at his hands. Father was toying with me, upping the ante before he moved in for the kill.

To prevent the last thread of my self-control from unraveling, I paced for an hour. I loathed myself for thinking I could provoke Father with no consequences. Finally, I sat in a corner of the office, beating my forehead on my knees, hating myself for such recklessness. How could I save that little girl? I couldn't think of a way to locate Grace.

Poor Lauren and Matthew. They must be insane with worry. Thinking of them multiplied the shame that eroded my resolve. *What did you do, Madisen? What did you do?*

Aunt Ceci's calm and reassuring words suddenly replaced my recriminations. *Worrying never did anyone any good. Fix it if you can. Then learn from it and move on.*

Fix it.

Okay, Madisen. Focus. I got to my feet and wandered through the house once more. Why would my father take Grace? Was I correct in presuming he was answering my message with one of his own? Since Angeline's death, my parents had resented me because they'd lost their favorite child, while I'd remained alive. And Angeline had said Father knew she'd loved me more.

And I loved her back fiercely. After she died, Aunt Ceci had become a mother to me and provided refuge. She'd given support, comforted me, and believed in me. She'd demonstrated more love in her little finger than both my parents combined.

But these thoughts didn't bring me closer to finding where my father might be hiding Grace. I was certain of only one thing: my hatred of him had no limits. If he harmed her, I'd rip him apart with my teeth if I had to.

At last, I sat on my bed, still wondering what to do.

****

Thursday, September 24

…The sun is newly risen, and the grass is wet with dew. We're playing hide-n-seek, and it's my turn to find Angeline. When we were children, she'd always hidden

so well I never found her. I'd have to give up and let her come to home base. She hadn't shown me her secret place before she died.

I check under the deck and in the bushes by the pond. I go to the front yard. She giggles.

"I heard that!" I yell. She's not behind the tree. There are no other places that could conceal her. "Where are you?"

Another giggle. The sound is close. Hearing movement, I whirl around to see her head rise from the ditch.

"Angeline! That's why I never found you. You were in the culvert under the driveway!"

"Yup!" she says triumphantly. "It's just big enough for me to wiggle into, feet first."

"I should've thought to look there." I'd never thought she'd risk encountering bugs or getting dirty.

She gives me an impish smile as we go inside. She dusts herself off and washes her hands, then joins me upstairs. My old bedroom is plain. One poster looks small on the otherwise bare walls. A couple of stuffed animals sit on the shelves crammed with books. I lie on the floor with my chin in my palms, and she lounges on the bed.

"What's wrong?" she asks.

"I've made a mess of things. Zac broke up with me, and now Father has kidnapped Grace because I challenged him."

"Why did Zac break up with you?"

I explained everything that had happened, saying, "I was stupid. I just wasn't thinking about the consequences of my message in the newspaper article. Now Zac's gone, and I've got to figure out how to get

Grace back."

"You didn't know Daddy would do that. It's not your fault. You just have to remember how mean he gets when he's mad."

I nod, seeing in her face she's afraid for Grace too. We both understand what our father is capable of...

Damn! I didn't mean to fall asleep. If Father had shown up, I'd have been a sitting duck. I listened for signs I wasn't alone in the house. I heard only silence. It was well after seven in the morning.

I dragged myself out of the bedroom and down the stairs. After making sure the curtains were drawn, I went to the kitchen. I started a pot of coffee, using lots of grounds to make it strong. I almost checked the refrigerator, barely remembering in time it was a bad idea. After two months, the food would be covered with slime.

A rummage through the pantry yielded only canned goods. None of it looked appealing for breakfast. I checked the freezer. Aha! A box of cheese danishes. I put two in the microwave to defrost.

A long day stretched ahead of me. I didn't worry about Sheriff Rey or Detective Hanson entering the house. They had no cause for a search warrant, and an officer wouldn't force an entry without one. And I didn't think my father would come until dark. Even so, I couldn't let my guard down. Surviving my father's attack and rescuing Grace would be the biggest tests of my life. Failing wasn't an option.

I got a big mug, filled it with coffee, and devoured the sweet rolls. I cleaned up the traces of my meal, poured myself another cup, and wandered around the second floor. To help me work through the impenetrable tangle of confusion my thoughts had become, I needed to go for a run.

I remembered buying my first pair of running shoes like it was last week.

At exactly eleven o'clock, Aunt Ceci had answered the front door. Zac came in, the January wind hurtling in behind him. I'd waited in the kitchen, trying to contain my excitement at shopping with him for an entire afternoon.

School would start again in four days, ending Christmas break. I hadn't been looking forward to the second half of my freshman year until Zac called that morning. He'd asked if I was going to try out for the track team in March.

"I hadn't thought about it," I'd answered.

"You've got speed. You'd be an asset. And after my training, there's no doubt you'll make the team."

The anemic sunshine didn't affect the winter chill, and I was grateful his car was warm. As he drove toward the city, he had me laughing at his locker room antics during football season.

"Are you going to play football in college?" I asked. He would graduate high school in May. I already dreaded his absence next year, wondering how I'd get through the day.

"You're sweet to think I could make the university team. I'm going for prelaw. I'll have to study a lot to keep my grades up. No time for organized sports."

Oak Arbor Mall in Woodland Park, Kansas, was the best place to go, he'd insisted, even though there were other stores closer. It would have the largest selection in one place. The crowded parking lot had been stripped of Christmas decorations, and post-

The Art of Being Broken

holiday bargain hunting was in full swing.

Before hitting the shops, we ate lunch in the food court. He told me to choose my favorite place, and I made a beeline for the pizza counter. I knew he liked spicy food, and I loved the double cheese. He insisted on paying, then devoured four slices as I nibbled on one.

"You're so slender. You're going to have to eat more once we get started."

"What exactly do you mean by 'training'?" I asked.

"To get you ready for the team tryouts, you'll do sprints to build power, distance runs for endurance, and lift weights to gain strength. We'll work on your form too. I think it's already pretty good, though. You're a natural."

"So, you're going to coach me?" I felt my eyes get big.

"Yeah. I mean, if that's okay."

"Sure," I said, hiding my huge grin by sipping my drink.

With lunch finished, we looked in the first store that carried running shoes. They only had two pairs in my size, and Zac said he didn't like the way they fit. We moved on to a specialty store for women's athletic footwear. Zac had the salesman measure my foot in my thick socks, and then asked him to bring every brand they had in my size. I tried on seven pairs. Of course, the most expensive one fit the best.

"Buy them," he encouraged. "They're going to take a beating. They'll have to be durable and comfortable. You can't train with blisters or sore feet."

The clerk rang them up for me. As we walked out of the store, Zac laced his fingers through mine. It was the first time he held my hand.

When school resumed, we started with the weight machine after he showed me how to warm up to prevent injury. When the weather wasn't too cold, he had me do distance runs outdoors, which was easier than the indoor sprints. They tired my legs until I thought I'd collapse.

"Again," Zac said after I'd walked around a minute to catch my breath. We were in the gym again after school. My muscles protested. I didn't grumble, not wanting Zac to think I was weak or didn't appreciate his help. For the tenth time, I pushed myself as hard as I could, sprinting to the end and back.

In the locker room, my stomach mutinied, and I threw up from the exertion. I showered and changed, and Zac walked me to his car. He gave me a hard look.

"You're pale. Were you sick?"

"I'm fine."

"Answer the question."

"Yeah. But I'm fine," I'd repeated.

"Jesus, Maddie, you never complain!" He threw up his hands when I didn't answer. "You've got to let me know if I'm pushing too hard. It's not beneficial to overwork your body. Next time, you have to tell me. Promise?"

"Okay," I said, knowing I wouldn't do it.

Tryouts came on March first. Zac watched from the bleachers by the track.

"There she is!" Randy Hess walked up to me as I joined the group waiting for the coaches. I'd never spoken to him. He was a junior, very popular, and one of the best sprinters in the state. "You ready?"

I nodded in answer, and he waved at Zac.

The trials were a breeze. I'd outrun all the girls in the quarter- and half-mile, except for one senior. The next day, Coach had posted the names of those who'd made the team, and I was second on the list. For the first time, I'd become part of a group and made friends at school. Randy coined the nickname "Mad Dash." He'd encouraged others to shut down snide remarks about me with harsh glares, creating a protective bubble.

Thanks to Zac.

Damn him! He ensured I'd be accepted by making me an asset to the team. He'd also asked Randy to look out for me. How had I overlooked it at the time? I owed him so much, and now he hated me. I rubbed my chin to wipe away the tears.

Chapter Ten

Leaving my empty cup on the bed, I sat on the floor of the upstairs landing. With the gun close by, I began stretching. After my muscles were warmed up, I did as many exercises as I could think of. Crunches, push-ups, leg lifts, and squats. Even jumping jacks. Anything to keep moving. But it was no substitute for running. I couldn't find my zone.

I grabbed an old jump rope from my bedroom closet and went to the wood floor downstairs. After some false starts, I was able to alternate feet the way boxers do. I found myself getting into the rhythm, and my mind's useless whirring slowed. I examined one issue at a time.

Last night, Angeline had revealed her secret hiding place. When she was alive, she didn't like messing up her clothes—she was much too girly. I never would've guessed she'd crawled into the huge pipe. I shook my head at her ingenuity.

She'd reminded me how malicious our father could be, especially when he was angry. It dawned on me he'd planned and carried out Grace's abduction in a matter of hours. What else would he do to punish me? Slipping into the house during the night to shoot me seemed too simple. I was naïve compared to his insidious cunning.

My thoughts veered to Bobby's son, Tony. Oh!

The Art of Being Broken

He'd told officers Auntie Elaine was the driver who'd hit Bobby on the night of the accident. The officers misunderstood him, thinking he'd said, "Auntie Lane."

I thought about what he'd told me in the hospital: "She's not really my aunt. That's what she wants me to call her." Why in the world would Elaine want Tony to call her "aunt"? Were they somehow related? Good God Almighty! Was Elaine his mother? Bobby had said the mother lived in Clantonville and never came to see him.

On that thought, with arms weak from exertion, I stopped jumping. The exercise had helped tremendously, and I felt better. All the same, I was no closer to predicting what Father might do next or where Grace could be. Heart pumping furiously and panting hard, I put the rope back where I'd found it and went to take a quick shower.

I toweled dry, got into clean clothes, and put the gun in my waistband. I raked through my wet hair with a brush from the vanity.

Now, it was a matter of passing the time until nightfall. I fingered the gun and went to the basement to be sure I was alone. Moving to the main floor, I checked the rooms. Restlessly, I roamed the house like a ghost unable to reconcile its memories of the past.

Looking outdoors, I stood to one side of the window to peer down the blacktop road. Angeline had stared out the same window on our tenth birthday.

The morning had been cloudy and windy. Angeline had stared as if trying to will the sun to come out. She'd fretted that our outdoor party would be spoiled. Ambivalent, I didn't want her to be disappointed, but I also wouldn't have cared if the party was canceled. The kids who'd been invited would mostly ignore me. I usually felt like an outsider around children my own age, never knowing what to say to them.

To Angeline's immense relief, the clouds had parted, and the sun was shining by two o'clock.

"They're here!" Angeline shouted when the doorbell rang. She opened it to Ashley Wagner, Nicholas Leister, and Heather Rhetkins. Only Nick said hello to me as Angeline led them to the gift table in the back yard. Soon, fifty more grade-school children were running and screaming on the lawn.

Inept at handling youngsters, Mother watched from a distance, drinking cola with vodka from a cup. Father took pictures, speaking only when someone got in the way of his shot of Angeline.

It was Miss Cecilia (she didn't become "Aunt Ceci" until after Angeline died) who took charge, organizing the three-legged race and a game of capture the flag. She saved playing tag for last and had me wait to be "it" until others had taken their turn. "Because," she'd explained with a wink, "no one can catch you."

When we'd burned our excess energy, she corralled us for gift opening and cake.

The three-layered confection she presented to "the birthday girls" was intricately decorated with colorful icing flowers on green vines with silk butterflies. I stared in awe. It was the most beautiful thing I'd ever seen.

Suddenly, I was yanked by the shoulder.

"Out of the way," Father snapped. Elaine and her best friend, Macy Harvey, saw my humiliation and sneered.

"Okay, Daddy, now with Maddie," Angeline had

said, putting an arm around my shoulders. Those two photos were the only ones taken of us together that afternoon.

Two days later, she was gone.

****

The weight of my broiling emotions tired me more than my physical exertions. The fatigue finally caught up with me. I decided to get some sleep so I could be alert throughout the night.

In Angeline's room, I stretched out on the bed but didn't drop off right away. I tried to relax by thinking of her. Sometimes, we had tickle fights. "Maddie! No," she'd squeal. "Stop!" Both of us crying with laughter, we'd collapse on the floor.

Each memory of her was sacred to me. I'd told no one about the details of our time together after she died. Once, I slipped and told Aunt Ceci I'd talked to her. Aunt Ceci's spoon had halted mid-air over the pot on the stove, and she'd given me the strangest look.

"What did you talk about?"

"How the kids at school tease me," I'd answered carefully. "I dreamed about her last night."

She gave me a hug. "I know you miss her."

"Yeah. I wish I really could talk to her." Leaving the kitchen, I hoped Aunt Ceci was convinced I didn't think seeing Angeline was real, though I knew it was...

I woke with a start. Shit! It was almost dark. I'd thought I'd be up long before then. I had to eat before my father arrived.

Dinner was another can of beef stew. I forced myself to eat it fast, and it made me feel queasy.

Then I waited. I avoided staring at the clock as I paced with the gun in my hand. I thought an hour must have passed. It was ten minutes.

If only I could rest my head on Zac's shoulder. I yearned to touch his body. To know he supported me. I wanted to see his beautiful chocolate eyes, darkening with desire when he looked at my lips. Why had I been so selfish? So wrapped up in my need to confront Father I forgot to think of him? Forgot there was an "us." I raked the back of my hand across my face, ashamed. *You got what you deserved. You're on your own now.*

How would I save Grace?

I recalled how Father had lashed out at me, in torment over Angeline's death. Though his love for her was vile, he had truly grieved. He knew sorrow. Understood my pain at losing Aunt Ceci. He would want to keep hurting me, to prolong my suffering. To make me lose even more.

What was left for him to take?

Her house. He would have read on the newspaper's website Aunt Ceci had given it to me when she died. All her possessions had been ruined by the vandalism. I'd been forced to throw them away. But I still had the house.

The message my father was sending me? Maybe I knew.

If I wanted to save Grace, I had to go to Aunt Ceci's.

****

The waiting was about to make me crazy, so I decided to test my theory. I stuck the gun in my back waistband and tied the key to Aunt Ceci's house into my shoelace. Listening as I went outside, I heard only the call of owls. All else was quiet at one o'clock in the morning. I ran the mile to the edge of town. In the residential neighborhood, a few tree frogs purred. There were no streetlamps. Scattered porchlights punctured the blanket of darkness.

I jogged without a sound, using tree trunks and parked cars to shield me when possible. From one street over, I army-crawled between the houses whose back yards bordered Aunt Ceci's, then crouched behind the shrubs. The house looked empty. Nobody peered through the door or disturbed the curtains.

A half hour passed before I found the courage to go in. *You're not ready to die.* I pushed the thought out, refusing to worry further about what could happen. I grabbed the gun and retrieved the key.

My heart thrashed as I went in the back door and locked it behind me. A light over the stove barely illuminated the empty kitchen. I crept to the living room. Father wasn't there. I felt my way to the bathroom, where a light was on. I checked both bedrooms. The house was clear.

In the spare bedroom, I knotted the key in my shoelace again with trembling hands. Deep breathing couldn't stop the fear that trickled over my skin. I heard a slow creak and strained to listen, scared my next move would be my last. No other sound followed, and I let out a lungful of air. Nerves would be my undoing if I didn't get them under control.

Shattering glass in the kitchen blew apart the quiet. I froze, my throat thick. Time seemed to slow.

More breaking glass, this time in the living room. Then a small thump. Why break the front window? Smashing a pane in the back door put the lock within reach. I remained motionless, waiting…

Then I smelled smoke.

Rushing forward in panic, I saw a glow in the kitchen doorway. The fire was growing fast. A small flame danced on the living room floor. It was a rag burning inside a bottle. I raced past it, unlocked the front door, yanked it open, and fled into the night.

Tearing down the middle of the street, I ran for two blocks before my brain switched on. I cut between houses and hid behind a storage shed. Panting loudly, I forced myself to breathe through my nose.

You could've been burned alive. Like a machete, shock carved my gut. If both Molotov cocktails had ignited, escape would've been impossible. The yowling of a cat wrenched my attention to the present. I skulked in the shadows, trying to control my wobbling legs.

The aura of flames grew brighter. Hadn't someone called the fire department? I reached for my phone, remembering I'd left it at Father's house. At last, a siren shrieked from far away. It was time to go.

I cut down alleys and side streets for eight or ten blocks. Continuing along the sidewalk, I picked up my pace. The wind felt cold on my sweaty skin. Alert for fire trucks and police cars heading to the blaze, I took a circuitous route through town.

My legs grew heavy as stone, and I began to weaken. I'd hit a wall from the adrenaline crash. The distance seemed impossible; one mile might as well have been a hundred. *You're not going to make it.* I focused on my legs, digging deep for the strength to take one dogged step at a time.

The gun was still in my hand; I'd forgotten about it. Damn. I had to get my shit together. If I didn't grow a brain, I'd fall prey to my father's next trap. I stuffed the revolver into my shorts and trudged on.

Once out of town, I looked back. The glow from the fire was clearly visible. I heard shouts made small by the distance. Every fireman, city police officer, and county deputy would be at the scene.

A hopeless whimper escaped my throat. Father had, yet again, outsmarted me and upped the stakes. Next time, it would cost me my life. Maybe I should go to Sheriff Rey. Tuck my tail between my legs and ask for help.

God damn it, Madisen. You're not giving up! I owed it to Angeline and Grace.

I owed it to myself.

Somehow, I couldn't let Father win.

Chapter Eleven

Although he'd failed to roast me alive, Father's plan was effective. No cavalry would be coming to my rescue. Every law enforcement officer's attention was on the fire. Yet again, he was one step ahead of me. Even so, I'd do my best to make it difficult for him. At his house, I went through the same routine of circling to the back. I watched behind the blackberry bushes for clues he was inside. He wasn't giving himself away.

I slipped in through the basement without a sound, watching and listening. The quiet made tendrils of dread curl over my skin.

Bile rose in my throat. *You can't shoot if you're puking.* Swallowing the acid, I slunk to the first floor like I was wading through quicksand. I was scared I'd find Father and scared I wouldn't. The tension was getting to me. I tightened my grip on the gun to steady my shaking. I peeked in every room, trying to shield myself with walls and furniture. No one was there.

I edged up the stairs, back to the wall. On the second floor, Angeline's room was down the hall, and my old room was closest to the steps. Without hesitation, I stalked in. He wasn't there. I checked the closet anyway.

The door to Angeline's room was shut. In the seconds it took to reach it, I couldn't remember if I'd left it open. Not pausing to think, I twisted the knob and entered, gun raised.

"Well, hello, Madisen." Cold metal jabbed my ear.

"Hello, Father," I said. To my surprise, my voice was steady. The confrontation had finally come, and he'd won. My fear evaporated. I'd die knowing I'd done all I could. "At least I'll get to see Angeline again."

"What?"

"I'll see Angeline. After you kill me. She's watching, you know."

"Toss your gun on the bed," he said. I obeyed and kept talking, hoping to upset him.

"You thought Mother was crazy. She's not. Angeline speaks to her. She visits me, too." I walked into the room and spun to face him. The ten weeks he'd been on the run hadn't treated him well. His chin was covered in a four-day beard, and his hair was greasy. Sallow skin drooped under haggard eyes filled with scorn.

"She knows it was you who shot at me Tuesday morning," I said.

His expression fell for a moment. He pinned it back in place, then sneered.

"Don't believe me?" I raised a mocking brow. "Monday night, Angeline told me you figured out Elaine wasn't Robert van Horne's daughter. You tormented Caroline, never letting her forget it."

He couldn't hide his surprise. "Nobody else knew that. How'd you find out?"

"I already said. I talked to Angeline."

"That's not true. She's gone," he stated, but his eyes showed a trace of doubt.

"Elaine and Caroline hated us. They made me and

Angeline miserable. I never knew why until a few days ago. It was because of you."

"You deserved it."

"Did Angeline deserve it? She hasn't spoken to you since she died, though you claim you loved her."

"I did love her! She was my Angel." He stormed toward me. I backed into the dresser.

"You don't know what love is." I snorted in derision. "You made her life hell. She loathed you."

"Shut the fuck up!" He raised the gun to my forehead.

"Don't move!" said a voice from the doorway.

Father jumped and glanced over his shoulder. Lauren pointed a handgun, squinting in hatred.

"Drop it. Let her go," she ordered.

"Lauren? What are you doing?" Father asked.

"Put the gun down."

"You don't want me to do that. Madisen could get away. She's the one who took Grace. It's her you want."

Would she believe his lie? I shook my head. "I would never hurt your little girl."

"I know you kidnapped Grace, Father. I said, put down the gun."

I choked on a gasp. *Wha—?* My mind went blank.

What did she say? *Father.* Lauren was…my sister?

I rejected the idea. Angeline was my sister.

"Madisen, I didn't mean to tell you yet." Remorse tinged her voice. "I was going to give you time. To be friends first. I hoped to be someone you wished were your sister."

I answered with a hostile stare.

Taking advantage of our distraction, Father

grabbed my wrist and yanked it behind my back. He jerked me in front of him and pinned me with the gun under my jaw. I struggled in his grip.

"Don't." His breath was sour. "The gun might go off. Wouldn't want that to happen, would we?"

I gritted my teeth to keep from gagging.

"Well, isn't this a cozy reunion? Lauren, you'll let me leave with Madisen."

"Shoot me," I told her. "The bullet will pass through and hit him too. He'll kill me anyway. He won't let you live either. You're a witness." The muzzle smashed my jugular vein, making my pulse thud against it.

"I swear I won't hurt you, Lauren. I have no reason to," he said.

"I don't believe you. Tell me what you've done with Grace."

I felt him tense. He was out of options.

"Where's Grace?" she snarled.

I was startled at her sudden change. She looked feral.

"If I knew, I would tell you. I didn't take her."

"Don't lie to me."

"I wouldn't lie."

The fabrication had barely left his mouth when his gun arced in her direction. I grabbed his arm, pulling as hard as I could.

There was a crack followed by a deafening boom.

****

A hand gripped my shoulder. From the floor, I looked up and saw Lauren's lips moving.

"I can't hear you."

"Are you okay?" she shouted.

"Yeah." She helped me sit up, and I looked around. Father had fallen on his side. I scuttled away from him. I didn't see a wound, but blood seeped into the carpet under his head. His half-opened lids showed only white.

He was gone.

Like a puppet with cut strings, Lauren crumpled beside me. "Now we can't find Grace!" Her head sank to her hands.

My mouth went dry. *Grace*.

I thought I heard a giggle. I rubbed my ear to stop the ringing.

Angeline chortled again. Yes. Father would have put Grace somewhere close by.

"Lauren?" She didn't answer. "Lauren!" I shouted. She raised her head, eyes helpless. "Where's your car?"

"Up the road a little way."

"Give me the keys."

"Uh, they're in it. In the coin slot."

"Do you have your phone?" She nodded, looking bewildered. "Call the police. You have to report this. If you leave, you'll be a suspect. You don't want to be charged with murder. Explain it was self-defense. Give them all the details."

"What?"

"I'm taking your car," I said.

"You're leaving?"

"Do it!" I leaped to my feet. "Make sure Sheriff Rey gets word I'll be at the Clantonville hospital in twenty minutes." I ran into the hall. "Tell him I'm bringing Grace."

I left Lauren yelling questions from the top of the stairs as I slammed the front door between us. *Please let Grace be okay*, I prayed. Skidding to my knees in

The Art of Being Broken

the ditch, I peered into the concrete tube under the driveway. The gloom was impenetrable. I scooted closer and felt inside. My hand met dust and crusty leaves.

She had to be here. I lay on my stomach and pushed until my shoulder was inside the culvert, reaching as far as possible. There was nothing.

"No!" I sobbed. Frantic, I ran to the other side of the conduit. Reaching in, I felt hair.

Thank God! "Grace? Can you hear me, sweetheart?" She didn't move when I touched her cheek. Placing my feet on each side of her head, I grabbed her under the arms and heaved her onto my legs. Her mouth, wrists, and ankles were duct taped.

"Grace, honey. Are you awake? Grace?" I called. No movement. I put two fingers on her neck. Her pulse was steady and seemed strong for a child of five. I picked her up, and she lolled against my arm.

Darkness swallowed us as I rushed to Lauren's sedan. It was parked with the passenger wheels off the road. I tried the door on that side, finding it locked. The driver's door opened, and I heaved Grace over the console. Her bound hands flopped onto her lap. I buckled her in and started the car.

Prayers repeated in my mind as I sped across town. A police cruiser pulled behind me, lights flashing. Lauren's message must have reached the sheriff's department. I stomped the gas. The car stayed on my bumper. After a few blocks, it passed me, and I saw Sheriff Rey behind the wheel. I trailed him to the hospital's emergency entrance.

Throwing the gear shift into park, I yanked open my door. Sheriff Rey tugged me into his arms. I clung to him. Nurses ran to the car with a stretcher.

"*Mija*," he said. He drew back to examine me, then hugged me again. I nearly dissolved into tears.

As Grace was wheeled inside, relief made me wilt. With a strange mix of anguish and elation, I realized it was over.

You survived. You found Grace.

****

Sheriff Rey still had his arm around me when a white truck screeched into the lot. Without bothering to cut the engine, Zac hurled himself out. He sprinted to me and seized me in his arms.

"I can't believe you're okay!" he said into my hair. "Why did you risk it? You could've been killed."

I stood with arms hanging limp as he switched between cupping my face and embracing me.

"It's none of your business," I said, wiggling. He squeezed me harder. "Let me go."

"I won't let you push me away. Why did you tell Tabs I broke up with you?"

"You yelled. You said you were done and left!"

"Oh, Maddie! I meant I couldn't discuss it anymore. I was terrified I'd lose you and needed time to simmer down. I wasn't walking out on you. I'll never do that." He kissed me, parting my lips with his tongue.

Euphoria consumed me. I had to taste and feel him again. Smell his delicious scent. I reveled in the warmth of his skin and his hands pressing me to his body. I needed all of him.

Zac and I were lost in each other a short two minutes when a hand patted my back. "Okay," Sheriff Rey said. "All right, you two. You can, uh…*talk* later." We were slow to come apart. Arms around each other, we walked to the door. Sheriff Rey took care of parking Zac's pickup.

After I'd given a nurse the few details I knew about Grace, Zac and I were shown to an exam room. I clasped his hand and held a cup with the other. The water rippled with my trembling.

"I don't need to see a doctor," I said. "I'm fine. It's just adrenaline."

"I'm sure you're right," Zac answered, "but I'd like you to get checked. Please?" When I nodded, he asked, "Do you want to stay until we get news about Grace?"

"Of course. I wonder if they'll let Lauren be with her?"

"I don't know. Dad only said your father was shot and you had Grace."

Before I could respond, a petite nurse came in. She introduced herself as Beth and took my blood pressure and heart rate.

"How is it?" Zac asked.

"Both are above the normal range," she said. "Nothing to worry about, given the excitement. Do you have other pain or injuries?"

"No, I'm just tired. How's the little girl I brought in? Do they know what's wrong with her?"

"The doctor is with her now," she said, typing notes in my file.

"How long before we find out why she won't wake up?" I ran a hand through my hair.

"She's getting a thorough exam. We may need to run tests. Try not to stress about it. She's in good hands."

A man came in. "Hello, I'm Doctor Bernard," he said, looking at the computer over Beth's shoulder.

"Ms. Chandler, what brings you here?"

"Nothing a little rest won't cure," I said. "Please call me Madisen. This is Zac. He wanted me to be looked over. I think he worries too much."

"Hi, Zac." To me, the doctor said, "He's right to err on the side of caution. I understand you brought in the girl who was abducted?"

"Yes. How's she doing?"

"No information yet. I see in the notes you were here last week with a concussion. Are you having headaches or pain in your shoulder? Any other injuries?"

"Nothing. The headache disappeared after five days. My shoulder was sore at first. It hasn't hurt at all lately." That was a stretch. My whole body ached.

He examined my scalp where I'd struck my head and manipulated my arm. "Does that cause discomfort?"

"Nope," I said. "It's good."

"Okay, Madisen. You're healing fine. Come back if you experience disorientation or unusual soreness. It was good meeting you both."

As soon as the doctor left, I was out the door. Zac and I joined his dad in the waiting area. "Any news?" Sheriff Rey shook his head. After a moment, I said, "Why aren't you asking me what happened?"

"Detective Hanson is on his way. You can give him a statement," Sheriff Rey said.

Zac squeezed my hand. "You can tell me later."

I ran my fingers through his disheveled hair, unable to keep from touching him. He wore a T-shirt that looked like he'd scooped it off the floor, with jeans and flip-flops. He kissed my palm when I rested it on his cheek.

The hospital clock read twenty minutes past four when Detective Hanson lumbered in. He nodded to Sheriff Rey and ignored Zac.

"Hello, Madisen." He was gruff. "Why don't you come along with me to the station." It wasn't a question.

"You can talk to her here, can't you?" Zac asked.

"Unless you're her defense attorney, you'll stay out of this."

"Defense attorney!" Zac yelled. "You're charging her?"

Chapter Twelve

Friday, September 25
"So, you hid Grace in the culvert, drove Tabitha Strayer's car to her workplace, and went to your father's house on foot. Was it your idea to kidnap the little girl or your father's? Did you plan to shoot him all along? Or did you have a disagreement?" Detective Hanson demanded.

My nostrils flared as I struggled to hold my temper. I'd related events since Tuesday morning in detail. Hanson's doubts rose after each hole he claimed to find in my story, starting with my failure to report being shot at and ending with my knowledge of where Grace had been hidden.

"I've told you a dozen times. I had nothing to do with kidnapping Grace."

Exhaustion leached into my bones. It seemed like days since I'd slept. My body groused. My head ached, switching between heaviness due to lack of sleep and vertigo from needing food. I sat on a wood chair that got harder by the second, in a tiny room at the sheriff's department. John Hanson had shut the door on Zac when he followed from the hospital.

A deputy with a crewcut and "Morris" stitched on his uniform sat in on the interrogation. The detective's large girth pressed on the recorder as he leaned over the table.

"You waited for your father to arrive. When he wasn't—"

"I didn't help him take Grace," I repeated.

"—there by one a.m., you jogged into town, set fire to the house, and ran back to your father's place." A vein bulged in his temple.

"What?" I cried.

It was his first reference to arson. Deputy Morris twitched wide eyes to Hanson.

"I cherish the memories of Aunt Ceci in that house. It's one of the last things I have of hers. I'd never destroy it!"

"You work in insurance," Hanson said. "I bet you bought a big policy on it, since you know how to game the system."

"It's still protected by Aunt Ceci's policy, and it's covered for less than my annual salary. She treated me like a daughter. Why would I destroy a gift from her? Why commit insurance fraud, risk my career and going to jail for such a small amount of money?"

"You tell me!" he shouted.

"All right, that's enough."

A lanky man in boots, jeans, and a white dress shirt stood in the open door. A bit of gray frosted his wavy blond hair, and he held a briefcase. Smile lines marked his face, though he wasn't grinning now. Under heavy brows, shrewd eyes assessed the room. "If you gentlemen will excuse us, I'd like to speak to Ms. Chandler."

"Who are you?" Hanson demanded.

"Webster Robinson," he answered. When we kept staring, he added, "Attorney."

"She hasn't called a lawyer," Hanson spat.

"Nevertheless, I am here." When the detective and deputy continued to gawk, the man stepped in and motioned to the door. "If you will."

Deputy Morris nodded at me as he rose. Detective Hanson nailed me with a glare, then followed his belly out of the room.

The lawyer closed the door and took a chair. "May I call you Madisen?"

I nodded.

"Great. Call me Web. Sorry I wasn't here earlier. Zac asked me to come. I didn't see his message right away and then had to drive from Jeff City."

"Zac called you?"

"Yes. He felt unqualified to defend you since he's never practiced criminal law. Too bad he didn't pursue it. He was one of my best students."

"You're a professor?" I asked, trying to catch up.

He nodded. "I'm semiretired. I like to handle a case now and then. Before I get you out of here, I'm supposed to give you a message. Sheriff Rey says Grace is fine. Aside from queasiness and a headache, she's completely unharmed."

I was powerless over my tears. "I'm sorry to be emotional. I was terrified she'd been hurt."

"No need to apologize, young lady. Sit tight. I'll be back in a minute."

From one side of the room to the other, I counted. The length was five steps. I don't know how many times I'd paced it when Web returned. He said I was free to go, and I went with him outside to his car.

Exhausted with all that had happened in the last fifty hours, it didn't occur to me I was leaving with a total stranger. I was just grateful to get away from the detective and his damning accusations. Web opened the door of his burgundy Cadillac for me.

"You hungry?" he asked as we pulled away.

"I could eat a side of beef."

His bark of laughter made me smile.

"I'm serious," I said. "Yesterday, I only had sweet rolls and a can of stew."

"They didn't give you breakfast?" He seemed dismayed. "I'll buy you lunch. What would you like?"

"It doesn't matter, as long as it's fast."

"Drive-through it is."

Not caring about my poor manners, I wolfed the burger, fries, soda, and milkshake in the car when it was handed to me.

Web parked in front of Zac's house. The second I stepped over the threshold, he trapped me in a viselike hug.

"I'm glad to see you too, but, uh…need to breathe here," I said.

Zac eased his grip and gave me a light kiss. "Are you all right?"

"I'm fine. Web treated me to lunch. I feel much better."

"Thank you, Web." Zac released me. "Shall we sit at the table?"

"We'll be more comfortable in the living room," Web said. He opened his briefcase and took out a small device. "Do you agree that I will represent you and I can record this conversation?"

"Yes, I agree," I answered.

"So, Madisen, tell me about this hubbub you've found yourself in. I want all the particulars." He winked at me like we were old friends sitting down to chat.

The accusations of arson and kidnapping frightened me, and I was grateful for his help. Without hesitation, I explained, "I'll have to start with my trip here in July. I came for Aunt Ceci's funeral. I hadn't spoken to my father in ten years. He cornered me at the cemetery and invited me to his house for dinner…"

Zac didn't speak in the hour it took to tell the story. He was surprised and angry when I described the gunshots on Tuesday morning. For his benefit, I emphasized I was sure my father wouldn't stop until he'd killed me.

Of course, I omitted the part about speaking with Angeline, though I didn't outright lie. And I left out that I'd learned who Lauren's father was. I didn't believe it was relevant.

Web occasionally interrupted to ask a question. He didn't miss a detail, and my confidence in his ability grew.

"Did Detective Hanson indicate what they might charge you with?" he asked.

"He said I'd worked with my father to take Grace, shot him, and set fire to Aunt Ceci's house."

"What?" Zac blurted. "That's ridiculous."

I shrugged, just as confused.

"Well, it looks like I have lots of work to do," Web said. "I'll look at your phone records and go to the hotel you checked into.

"If Lauren agrees, I'll take her statement of events the night your father was shot. Unfortunately, the accusation of arson may be difficult to disprove. You admitted to being in the house when the fire started. Hanson's theory about collecting the insurance money is weak. I'll poke around to see if the neighbors saw anyone."

He placed the recorder in his briefcase and stood. "Get some rest, Madisen. I'll be in touch." He shook our hands and left.

Zac helped me up from the couch. "We've got a lot to talk about, but you look like you're going to pass out. If you want to take a shower, I'll find clothes for you to sleep in."

"Thank you," I said, in no hurry to have the inevitable discussion.

Hot water dribbling over my skin felt divine. Zac left a pair of drawstring shorts and a T-shirt on the bed. Dropping the towel on the floor, I put them on and climbed between the sheets.

"I called Dad," Zac said when he came in a second later. "Lauren is taking Grace home."

"That's wonderful. I was scared Father might have—" I fell asleep mid-sentence.

...In her room, Angeline throws her arms around me. I hug her fiercely, relieved to see her again.

"I'm glad you're okay, Maddie," she says. "I was scared when Daddy pointed his gun at you. You're lucky Lauren showed up."

"I didn't need Lauren. I would've figured a way out of it."

She tilts her head at me, brows raised. I don't say more. She gestures to the blood-stained carpet. "Daddy was shot."

It hits me then. She's never expressed anger at Father for his abuse. "Aren't you mad about what he did to you?"

"I was, but not anymore. I forgave him. You should, too."

"He wanted to kill me, Angeline." I sigh. "You're asking a lot."

"I know you'd be happier if you did. I don't want you to turn bitter." When she understands I'm not going to answer, she says, "Lauren seems nice."

I throw daggers at her with my stare.

She shrugs. "Just saying..."

****

"Why didn't you tell me your plans for your father?" Zac asked. The time had come for one of the many "serious talks" I saw in my future.

Oh, boy.

Evening had fallen by the time I'd woken up, and I'd been starving. Zac cooked spaghetti because I didn't want to go out. Inquisitive townspeople were bound to interrupt us, demanding information about the shooting and the fire. Or worse, they'd treat me as if I was the criminal. I didn't have the energy to deal with it.

After dinner, Zac led me to the couch. I mentally squirmed at having to explain myself, uncertain he'd understand.

"You're right. I should have," I responded.

"If you'd let me—Wait, huh?"

"I said you're absolutely right."

"Okaaay." He looked at me like I'd grown two heads. "Why the change of heart?"

"You said once you should protect me. I agree. You'll need to come home with me to San Antonio. If you're with me twenty-four seven, I'll be safe."

"I see where you're going with this. I know I can't watch over you all the time," he said. "This was different. When there's a specific threat, you can't expose yourself even more. I was insane with worry.

What hurt me the most is you didn't talk to me about it. I know you're tired of me saying this, but it makes me think you don't trust me. And when you're reckless, it's like you're oblivious to how it affects me when you get hurt."

I bit my tongue to keep quiet about his trust issue and the "reckless" insult. "I understand your need to protect me," I said. "It was one reason I did it."

"That doesn't even make sense."

"Hear me out?" When he didn't answer, I asked, "Please?"

"All right," he said, crossing his arms.

"First of all, my father was determined to kill me. He was firing at me on the street. If you or a member of the family had tried to keep me safe, they would've been in danger of getting shot. Do you think I could've lived with that? I had to protect everyone."

"You know—"

"Let me finish, please. Second, I can't stay here forever. Eventually, I'd have gone home to Texas, and Father would've followed me. Then what would happen? I'd have been a walking target, living in fear, not knowing when I'd be gunned down.

"Third, I admit, my plan was a gut reaction." I added air quotes, " 'Reckless' as you call it. I had to make my own decisions and act on them to defend myself. Internalize the fact I'm not under his control or a helpless victim. I hope you can understand that."

He started to speak. I held up my hand, and he motioned for me to go on. "One last thing. It wasn't about trusting you. It was knowing what your response would be. If I'd talked to you about it, you'd have become 'superhero protector' and stopped listening.

You'd have refused to understand I needed to free myself from the past. You wouldn't have given me your support."

Zac opened his mouth. He shut it, jaw tense. A long minute passed before he took a deep breath and shook his head, looking disappointed. "That's the problem with you."

"What?" I asked. It would gut me if I lost him over this.

"You understand me too well," he said, placing a hand behind my neck. "That's exactly what I would've done."

Boneless, I sagged into his embrace, struggling to halt my thankful tears. "I meant it when I said you were right. I'm not used to putting another person first." Feeling his heartbeat gave me the strength to express my feelings. "I missed you. Those two days I thought you'd left me were agony. When you're there to reassure me, I can be strong. I wanted to see your smile or hear you scold me because you're losing patience. To have your arms around me like this."

"I need you too, baby." He kissed my head. "I was angry you didn't talk to me. But why would you if I refused to listen? I'm sorry."

"Apology accepted," I said.

"For the record, though, if you put yourself at risk, I'll try to stop you."

"If you'll listen to my reasons for wanting to do it, I'd say that's fair."

"I promise."

I took a deep breath. Now for the hard part. "I also decided to confront my father because I'd made a promise. For Angeline's sake, I swore to get revenge for what he'd done. I know that makes me a terrible person. If you can't live with that..." Tears blocked my throat.

He didn't respond. In the thick silence, his chest tightened and his whole body tensed. Gritting my teeth, I waited for the worst. He was trembling. When I tried to pull away, he held me tighter.

I realized he was laughing. *Laughing* at me. "God, Maddie," he said, rolling us onto the couch. I propped myself up, hands against his chest.

"What is it you find so hilarious?" I raised a brow. After a minute, he almost had himself under control. Then, with one look at me, he was chuckling again.

"You're ridiculous sometimes. It's normal to want vengeance for what your father did. I know you. You're not a vindictive person. You challenged him because he pushed you to it."

"Maybe you're right." I snuggled into his arms again. "So, you think I'm ridiculous, huh?"

"Yes," he said. "You're absurd if you think I'll ever let you go. And if you try to leave me, it won't work. I'll follow you around day and night, sad and pathetic, till you feel sorry for me and take me back."

"I doubt you could be pathetic if you tried."

"Baby, to keep you in my life, I'd go to the ends of the earth."

Relaxed, I stretched out, nestling my face into his neck, inhaling as he exhaled. He ran a leisurely fingertip along my arm, tracing slow circles to my shoulder. No one else touched me this way, as if my skin held secrets only he could reveal. I let out a sigh as he stroked along my throat and combed through my hair. He slowed each time until I yearned for the next caress.

I shifted to lie on top of him and got lost in his eyes. Their gentleness made my heart leap. I lowered my mouth to his, grazing it before moving up to kiss his forehead, his brows, his lids, jaw, and cheeks. He turned to capture my lips, teasing with his tongue. The taste of him made me moan. I opened to deepen our kiss, running my hands over his shoulders.

He was perfect. Smooth skin over rigid muscle that rippled with definition. I'd never tire of his body. I pulled up his shirt to run my thumb across his stomach, feeling his abs respond to my touch. He groaned and sat up, holding me to him. I wrapped my legs around his waist, and he carried me to the bedroom.

"I can't wait another second to make love with you," he whispered.

Chapter Thirteen

I nipped his bottom lip, then licked it. He sat me on the bed and rose to pull his shirt off.

"Wait," I said. "Stand still." I leaned back on my elbows, admiring the ridges of his abs and his narrow hips. His low-slung jeans barely covered the tantalizing V of his torso. A thin line of hair disappeared behind the button. I rubbed my thighs together. "Please, take them off."

Holding my gaze, he unzipped the fly and pushed them to his ankles, again standing to let me look at him.

"All of it," I breathed.

He pushed off his briefs.

His impressive erection made my mouth water. I let my stare travel over every plain and valley of his flesh, then settle on his cock. He was flawless.

"Take off your clothes," he said. I stood to pull off my T-shirt and shimmy out of the shorts. "Damn." He took his time inspecting my nakedness. "You're stunning. Every time I look at you, I want to be inside you."

"Touch me," I begged.

He knelt on the floor, running his fingers from my ankles to my waist, then skimmed my belly. As he brushed my nipple, I arched into him.

"You're so sensual. It kills me how you respond to my touch."

I lifted his hand to kiss his palm. "I love your hands on my body."

He trailed a string of kisses from my knee to my hip. "What about my mouth? You like it, baby?"

"Yes," I gasped. "I love your lips. I want your tongue."

He kissed his way to my slit and licked me. I couldn't hold in my shout of pleasure.

His fingertips replaced his lips, grazing along my slick opening and up to brush my clit. He rose to skim my breast with his tongue and flicked the hard peak.

I sucked in a breath at the searing heat in my center and grew wetter. He teased both erogenous zones at once.

He moved away, and I huffed at the loss of contact. "Lie on the bed," he said. When I did, he gripped my calves and pulled my butt to the edge. He lapped at my clit before sliding two fingers into me as his other hand caressed my nipple.

My God! The slight friction made me yearn for more. Soon I was begging, seeking my release.

"Not yet, baby," he said, taking his hands away.

I moved up to the pillow. "Come here."

He crawled onto the bed and rolled to his back. I straddled his legs and kissed him deeply. He swallowed my groan. I moved my lips down his body, reveling in the sweetness of his pecs and his abs. I nibbled his hipbone.

When I took his beautiful cock into my mouth, he hissed. Holding it firmly, I smoothed my tongue over his length. I took him into my mouth again until he hit the back of my throat.

"Oh, fuck!" he muttered.

Scratching my nails up his thighs, I worked him in and out, sucking and licking. His erection grew bigger, and he bunched the sheets in his fists.

"Stop, Maddie," he said, twitching in his effort to remain still.

I shook my head and kept going until he grasped me under the arms to pull me away.

"I have to be inside you. Now." Grabbing a condom from the bedside table, he sat up and sheathed himself. Putting a pillow against the wall to lean on, he turned me around. Facing away from him, I was pulled snug to his chest. As he guided his cock into me, I screamed at how good it felt. He didn't stir, and I wiggled my hips, panting in frustration.

He lifted my knee and massaged my clit.

"Oh, Christ. Please. Zac, make me come."

"I will, baby." He made a slow circle with his hips, moving in and out a fraction.

I hummed with insatiable desire, and he growled low.

"Touch yourself for me," he said.

My hand flew between my legs as he concentrated on teasing my nipple.

"Yes," I sighed. "Yes…" I squeezed my inner muscles.

"Fuck," he ground out. "You're gonna make me lose it."

I clasped my muscles once more.

He dug his fingers into my waist and lifted me, letting his cock glide out like a slow tide. He pushed into me inch by exquisite inch, making me delirious. His unhurried repetitions teased, winding me up until I was frantic.

"Say my name, baby. I love hearing you beg."

"Zac, I'm so close," I pleaded. "Zac. Please." Burning through space and time, I floated in a womb of hunger and unbearable anticipation.

He gradually accelerated the rhythm to a pounding tempo. Pressure coiled inside, building, tightening…

I burst into rapture. With a powerful climax, I cried, "Zac, don't stop!"

He continued driving into me. Orgasmic spasms whipped through my body over and over until I was chanting his name. Rumbling low in his throat, he thrust deep and pulsed inside me, pouring out his hot release.

Limp and dazed, I was supported in his arms as he ran his teeth over my neck.

"You're incredible, baby. I— That was amazing."

A weak, "Uh huh," was all I managed. Every drop of energy was gone. He chuckled, letting me rest on his lap as he nuzzled my hair.

Zac eventually went to get me a glass of water. He brought his phone when he returned. "There's a message for you," he said.

I read the text:

Tabs: —*Is Maddie there?*—

Zac: —*Yep.*—

Tabs: —*WTF, Maddie? You'd better have a good reason for not telling me what's going on. The rumors are out of control. I don't know what to believe. At least let me know you're okay.*—

Me: —*I'm in one piece. Exhausted. Let's get together tomorrow to talk.*—

Tabs: —*Fine.*—

"I'm in trouble," I said.

"What's up?"

"Tabs is mad because I haven't been in touch."

"She'll get over it."

"Easy for you to say. You don't have to answer to 'Tsunami Tabitha.' "

He got into bed and held me. Despite my worry over Tabs's irritation, I soon drifted off.

****

Saturday, September 26

It seemed I'd slept only a minute when a loud boom woke me.

The door bounced off the wall and slammed shut. "Hellfire, Maddie! You get out of that bed right now!" Tabs glared at me, hands on her hips.

"What are you doing here?" I spluttered, half awake.

"Zac let me come in as he was leaving. Get your ass up!"

"Why aren't you at work?"

"It's Saturday. I took yesterday and Thursday off to spend with my best friend. She seems to have forgotten."

Uh-oh! She had a right to be mad. "I'll explain," I said. "Let me get dressed."

"Hurry up." She stomped out of the room.

I showered fast, using Zac's shampoo and razor, and threw on a pair of his shorts and a T-shirt. Tabs was waiting for me on the couch, arms crossed.

I went to the kitchen. "You want coffee?" I started a pot.

"No, thank you," she answered stiffly.

Waiting as long as I dared, I poured myself half a cup and sat beside her. "I'm sorry I didn't let you know sooner I was okay. After the police released me, I had a long talk with my lawyer. By then, I hadn't slept for almost forty-eight hours. It was impossible to keep my eyes open a second longer."

"My God, Maddie. They arrested you?" she hollered, her hands dropping to her lap.

"I wasn't charged with a crime. Yet." I told her everything that had happened, adding the same reasons I'd explained to Zac. She was quiet until I finished.

"So, you lied to me," she said, nostrils flared.

I started to protest but thought better of it. "Yes," I admitted. "I lied about going with Amber and Tony to visit Bobby. I drove to the hospital in your car and ran into them while I was there. And I gave you the impression I was staying in the hotel close to the airport, which wasn't true, either. I'm sorry. I didn't want you to have to lie to Zac and Sheriff Rey. Most of all, I lied because I couldn't let you get hurt trying to help me."

"You didn't tell me you wanted to use my car because Zac broke up with you. And you didn't tell me your plans about baiting your father."

"No," I whispered. She flushed even more.

"Damn it, Maddie," she said, pointing at me. "Your father was out for blood. You might've been killed!"

"I had to do it, Tabs. I thought you would understand I had—"

"No. I don't understand. Friends share things like this. They talk about life-changing decisions or when they're getting into dangerous situations. Friends are supposed to be there for each other. I thought of you as family. Apparently, you don't think of me that way. Christ Almighty! You could have died!" She marched to the door and yanked it open. "Saying you're sorry isn't good enough." Before I could open my mouth, she left.

It was only eleven o'clock in the morning, and I felt like I'd been run over by a freight train. Lacking the energy to cry over Tabs's anger, I wiped my tears and wandered back to the bedroom to lie down. I noticed shopping bags on the floor. They contained two bras with matching panties, a pair of jeans, and two cute tops. They were from the store where Tabs worked. She must have dropped them when she flung open the door.

Sleep would've eluded me, so I put on the undergarments, jeans, and one of the tops. To Tabs's credit, everything fit perfectly. I decided to walk to Zac's office downtown. It would give me a chance to calm down and think of a way to ask Tabs to forgive me. I forgot everyone I ran into would demand information about the shooting and house fire that had rocked the sleepy little town.

No sooner had I stepped out the door than Jayce Phelps came up the walk. "Madisen. Good morning. How are you today?" he asked.

"Hello, Jayce," I said. Unhappy to see him, I didn't beat around the bush. "What can I do for you?"

"I wanted to talk to you about the goings-on yesterday." He seemed unfazed by my bluntness. "Both incidents are connected to you."

"I can't discuss open investigations. And I don't want to be the subject of public scrutiny." Surprised at myself for admitting as much, I added lamely, "Sorry." It was unkind. After all, he'd published an article when I'd asked. Yet the thought of the community's judgment made me shudder.

"I can appreciate how you feel." He inclined his head. "When you were growing up, your parents drew attention, and it wasn't the good kind. I think you'll find folks would be open to hearing your side of things. It could change their minds."

"I'm not sure about that. Once people pass judgment, they won't listen to a different point of view."

"Some," he conceded. "But if what I suspect is the truth were told, most would be sympathetic."

"I'll think about it," I said. "Now, if you'll excuse me."

"Need a lift? I can drop you anywhere in town," he offered. I almost refused, afraid he would continue to pester me with questions. Just then, Gwendolyn Hayes drove by. She craned her neck to stare at me. For years, she'd been Caroline van Horne's partner in spreading juicy gossip.

"That's nice of you. I'll accept the offer."

In the car, Jayce didn't try to interview me. Instead, he chatted about the weather and his hopes the high school football team would keep up their winning record. When he dropped me off on the town square, I thanked him for the ride.

"You're most welcome, Madisen. You take care of yourself." I darted into the hardware store. Zac's office was on the second floor of the building, the stairway tucked behind a door in the rear. I avoided browsing customers by skirting the tool display. A young man at the register said hello. I responded with a casual wave, not slowing. Taking the stairs two at a time, I almost bowled over an elderly man in suspenders and a baseball cap.

"Excuse me. I'm sorry," I muttered. Racing down the hall, I barged into the empty lobby and through the open door of Zac's office.

"Maddie," he said, sounding surprised. "What's wrong?"

I burst into tears.

He quickly shut the door and led me to his leather chair. Pulling me into his lap, he kissed my temple. "What is it?"

"Nothing," I sobbed, knowing it sounded ludicrous. "Everything!"

"Shh," he soothed. He rubbed my back as I muffled my wails. "Tell me what's gotten you this upset."

How could I articulate that my whole world was askew? "I tried to explain to Tabs," I blubbered. "But she won't forgive me. Nobody's going to when they f-find out how much I lied to them."

"Who won't forgive you, baby?"

"Sheriff Rey, th-the whole family."

"Dad's upset, but that won't last long. Aside from him, nobody else knew the details. I talked to Uncle José and Carlos this morning and let them know you're okay."

"I could go to jail, and Father t-took Grace, and he was shot. And Lauren is…She said she's…" A new flood of tears washed my cheeks. I couldn't voice it. It was too strange, too bizarre.

"Your sister," Zac finished, cradling my head on his shoulder. "Shh. You've been through so much. It's hitting you all at once. I promise it'll get back to normal soon."

His words made me sob even more. Reality had shifted. I was afraid I'd never feel normal again. "I think I hate her," I whispered.

****

Later that afternoon, Zac went to answer his door while I stayed slumped on his couch. Web came in with my suitcases, saying, "Hello."

"Come in. Make yourself comfortable." Zac motioned him to sit with me, then took my luggage to the bedroom.

Web looked me over. I had puffy eyes and a red nose. A soft "Hi there" was all I could get out. The tears hadn't abated after Zac brought me home, and I'd spent the entire afternoon crying.

"Maddie could use some cheering up. Do you have any news?" Zac asked. He brought a chair from the dinette set to the living room.

"Yes, I came by to tell y'all what I've learned," Web said. "First, I verified your phone records show no contact with your father, Maddie. Then, I went to the hotel. The manager let me review their computer and security systems. They confirm you came in at two minutes after three o'clock. Since it's impossible to get to Grace's school in seven minutes unless you can teleport, you weren't there when your father took her." Web chuckled at his joke about quantum physics. When I didn't join him, he added, "So, there is no evidence you had a part in Grace's kidnapping."

I nodded, encouraged.

Web clasped his hands. "And I found out something even better. Your account of the shooting got me wondering: how was it Lauren so perfectly timed your rescue? I contacted her to see if she'd speak with me. She was anxious to help."

Rescue? I tried to keep my smile from changing to

a snarl.

"We met this morning." Web leaned forward. "She'd read the article about your intention to rent your father's house and guessed what you were doing. When Grace was abducted by a man fitting his description, she decided to stake out his place. She followed you when you jogged to town. She parked down the street from your house and saw you run out when the fire started. She lost you after that, so she waited again at your father's property and saw you come back.

"Here's where it gets interesting. Lauren saw a man throw the Molotov cocktail through the living room window."

I felt my jaw drop. "Who was it?"

"She didn't see his face. It was too dark. He was a big man. 'Three to three hundred fifty pounds' is how she described him. Now, we have an eyewitness stating a large male threw an incendiary device right before you escaped the fire." Web gave me a grin. "I already talked to the detective. In light of this information, Hanson agreed not to pursue charges."

Wow! The grin that spread over my face was the first I'd worn all day. But my relief was short-lived.

Zac cleared his throat. "We might have a problem."

Chapter Fourteen

"What do you mean?" Web asked.

"About Lauren." Zac glanced at me.

"It's okay to tell him," I said.

"As a witness, she might not work in Maddie's favor. They're half sisters."

"Oh. I must've mixed that up. I thought she was your half sister."

"She is. Lauren is a half sister to both of us," Zac confirmed.

Web looked perplexed.

"And the answer is no, Maddie and I aren't related."

Web followed Zac's gaze to me.

I clarified, "Zac's parents are Deborah and Rey Redondo. My parents are Jacqueline and Clyde Chandler. Lauren's mother is Deborah. Clyde is her father; I didn't know I had another sister until she accidentally called him 'Father' when she told him to drop his gun." Crossing my legs, I looked at the floor. Not in the mood to discuss how Lauren had saved my life, I was also embarrassed to admit I'd skipped telling him she was my sister. "I'm sure Father kept the child he had outside his marriage a secret to protect his reputation."

"So, your parents, Clyde and Jacqueline, how long had they been married when Lauren was born?" Web asked.

"They'd been married five years when Angeline and I were born. Lauren is a year and a half older. So, it was three and a half years."

"Well, Lauren comes across as sincere and likable," Web said. "The fact she wanted to protect the sister who didn't know they were related could hurt either side. It depends on the jury. I doubt the prosecution will take the risk. As far as the detective is concerned, you're free and clear, Maddie."

"That's wonderful!" Zac said. "Isn't it, baby?"

My drifting attention was brought back to the men in front of me. "Uh, yes. Thank you, Web. I appreciate your help." I offered my hand.

"You're welcome," he answered, shaking it.

"Web, I'll walk you out," Zac said.

****

No answer came from Tabs after I texted her to say I was sorry once more. Apparently, her temper hadn't cooled as I'd hoped.

All the weeping I'd given in to during the afternoon had made me listless. Assembling a coherent thought required too much effort. I rooted through my suitcase for pajamas and put them on. Though it was early, Zac came to bed and held me. I slept peacefully in his arms.

...Angeline skips across the deck with the jump rope I'd found in the closet. It's early morning. The sun hovers over the horizon behind me as I sit on the rail.

"I don't think you're being fair," she says.

"About what?"

"To Lauren. When Daddy shot at her, you yanked his arm away. It saved her life. Now you won't even

talk to her."

I fist my hands in my lap and look away. "I'm not being unfair," I say. "I just don't think I'll have time. I'm leaving in a few days, and I've got a lot to sort out."

"She's waited her whole life to have a sister. She always wanted to know us, and Daddy wouldn't let her. It'll hurt her feelings if you don't talk to her."

"What about my feelings, Angeline?" I huff. "I don't want her. You are my sister."

"Of course, I'm your sister. That'll never change, silly. But Lauren never got the chance to have one. Ever. She had to grow up by herself. She was lonely. And she's sad right now. For a long time, she's wanted another baby. You can tell her it'll be okay."

"Well, I don't need her, and I don't want her."

Angeline stops jumping, puts her hands on her hips and shakes her head at me...

****

Sunday, September 27

When I shuffled into the kitchen, the smell of fresh coffee lit the receptors in my brain. Zac gave me that beautiful smile and offered me a cup. "How are you doing, gorgeous?"

"Better now," I said, blushing. "Thank you. You're the best boyfriend ever." I kissed his cheek, knowing my whole face would be swollen from my crying jag yesterday. Not "gorgeous" in the least; I must've looked like an ogre.

"You're welcome." He sat on the couch with me and ran his fingers through my hair. I had a hangover from melancholy. I was ashamed I'd given in to self-pity and let it sweep me away. Well, I wasn't going to

The Art of Being Broken

let it get the best of me again.

Zac went to the bedroom and came back after a minute. "It's for you," he said.

I took his phone, relieved Tabs had relented and was speaking to me again. "I'm glad you called," I said.

"Really? I was afraid you wouldn't be ready to talk."

The voice didn't belong to Tabs. I pulled the screen away from my ear, seeing Lauren was the caller. Zac received one of my dirty looks.

"—a shock to find out we're sisters. I wanted to apologize that you had to hear it under those circumstances. I intended to tell you while you were in town and pictured having a conversation to ease you into it. It all happened so fast."

"How's Grace doing?" I asked to change the subject.

"Oh, she's great. She can't wait to meet you. I explained Grandpa picked her up from school to take her for ice cream. When she got sick and needed to go to the hospital, her brand-new aunt Madisen drove her there. Since Matt and I were with her when she woke up, she wasn't scared. She doesn't remember much and seems unfazed. He'd drugged her with Rohypnol, and she slept through the whole thing."

"Do you think the experience will be detrimental? In the long run, I mean."

"I hope not. I'm watching for signs of trauma, and she hasn't demonstrated the common behaviors."

"Thank goodness. I was afraid he'd hurt her."

"Thanks to you, Grace is safe and sound. I'm going to see a child psychologist tomorrow. If Grace has questions in the future, I want to address them properly."

"You're a good mother."

"God knows I try. Matthew wants to thank you in person. Would you like to get together?" Before I could think of an excuse, she added, "It would mean a lot to us." Not wanting to disappoint Grace, I hesitated.

"Tell her she's invited to dinner tonight," Zac said.

"Zac's inviting you to dinner." As I spoke, I was planning how to dodge Lauren by persuading Tabs to spend the evening with me.

"That sounds great! Where and what time?"

"I'll let you discuss it with him." I handed Zac the phone. He went to the kitchen to finish the conversation, and I lumbered back to the bedroom and put on my running gear.

"I'll be back in an hour," I said to Zac.

"Have a good run. Please don't push yourself too hard."

I kissed him, grateful for his concern.

After warming up with stretches, I hit the sidewalk. It was a pleasant day, though my attention wasn't focused on the weather. I needed to sort through the jumble in my head.

Mary Anne, my therapist, would sometimes ask me to pick one word to describe my feelings about a person or situation. She said it prompted emotional regulation in the brain and decreased anxiety. I hated doing it, though I didn't admit it to her. It was difficult to label my scattered emotions. Sometimes it took days to settle on the right word. I'd also never told her the process helped.

Today, I had an hour. Hopefully, a condensed version of the assignment could compartmentalize my worries and slow the emotional rollercoaster. As my feet pattered a steady cadence, I tried to blank my mind. The first issue that popped into my head was Father. I inhaled deeply as I kept my strides long. Picturing him in my mind, I searched for the appropriate word.

He was gone. He'd hurt me for the last time by forcing me into a situation of kill or be killed. It was gratifying to remember him on the floor of Angeline's bedroom, his life draining away. Maybe I should've been alarmed at how little shame that brought me. I wasn't. He'd received his just deserts.

Resentment was my feeling about losing Aunt Ceci's house. For me, it held memories of her love. I'd never be able to relax in the room that held her favorite chair or sit in the kitchen where we'd talked over coffee. I wondered a moment who my father had hired or coerced to start the fire.

Elaine took me a while. Narrowing it down to two words for now, I picked disgust as one of them. Her attempt on my life was sickening. However, I also felt pity for her. After two days without him, I knew it was devastating to lose Zac.

Handsome and strong, his face stuck in my head. Dependable and thoughtful. Caring.

Love.

WHAT? You really have gone crazy. Did I love him? Was I capable of a forever kind of love? I loved Angeline and Aunt Ceci, as well as Sheriff Rey and the Redondo family. Still, I wasn't certain I could do a long-term intimate relationship. And when Zac found out Angeline and I communicated, he might not want to stay. It was too soon to worry about love.

Over the next two miles, I settled on alien as the

label for Lauren. I couldn't accept anyone other than my twin as a sister. It was wrong. And while the logical side of me understood Lauren wasn't to blame, I couldn't make sense of it. Like trying to describe a color outside the eye's visible spectrum, it was impossible.

A car door opening ahead yanked my attention to the woman stepping into my path. I recognized Caroline van Horne's bleached-blonde hair. I moved into the grass of the Langford's yard and quickened my pace.

"Madisen, wait," she said, holding her arm out to block me. I planted my feet and stumbled to avoid bumping into her. As if she were at a loss, she didn't say more.

"Well?" I asked.

She adjusted her suit jacket with manicured hands. In my whole life, I'd never seen her look uncertain. "I'd like to have a word with you," she said at length. "I wanted to appeal to your strong sense of compassion." She stood like a commander, sniffing as if empathy were a foreign concept.

Then, I was the one who hesitated. I couldn't imagine what she might want from me. Curiosity overcame my common sense, and I nodded.

"About Elaine's…behavior. You see, she became distraught after Zac broke all his promises to her."

I held up my palm, still catching my breath. "Zac didn't make any promises to Elaine, Mrs. Van Horne. Against my better judgment, I'll hear what you have to say. But if one more lie comes out of your mouth, you won't get another chance."

She gave me an appraising look, then wilted. I

never thought I'd see the day she behaved without pretense. "All right. Let me start over by saying Elaine's distress is genuine. She's had her heart set on marrying Zac since grade school. He ignored her until last year. During the weeks they dated, her possessiveness became alarming. When he broke it off, she was at her wit's end. Desperate.

"Then Zac started seeing you. It damaged her. She became irrational. Her dream had come true, then was snatched away by a person she despised. Surely you can understand the difficulties she was going through?"

She swept her gaze over me. I didn't answer. She continued, "I've tried to bring her out of this compulsion she has to pursue him. Nothing has worked. It's a fixation."

"She's been stalking him. And me," I said. Leaves rustled as the breeze picked up.

"Yes," she admitted, pursing her lips at the term. "I understood it was more than hurt feelings when she broke into—" She stopped short, giving me a miserable look.

It took a second to understand what she was going to say. "Aunt Ceci's house. She was the vandal." The insight gave me a shock. It shouldn't have.

Caroline nodded. "Please. You know it's not like her."

It was mostly true. Aside from the cat in my school locker, Elaine and her mother hadn't gone beyond talk. Yet wasn't that enough? Used as weapons, words could hurt. I'd been wounded by the shrapnel of gossip, spread for that very purpose.

"Do I?" I marched to the sidewalk. "I endured rumors insinuating I had a hand in Angeline's murder or was glad she died. It cut me deeply, and I was innocent. Until a few days ago, I had no clue you were doing it to get back at my father."

Her makeup didn't hide that she'd gone pale. Staring at her shoes, she had good reason to worry.

"Yes, I'm aware Elaine's biological father wasn't your husband. And I know about Tony Wittford." I waited until she looked up. "You think I'd pass up this opportunity? Let go of my chance to punish you for the pain you caused?" The question hung over her like the blade of a guillotine. "Let me give you the answer. I'm not you, Caroline. I don't give a shit. I don't spread rumors or try to elevate myself by bringing others down. Especially children."

I glared at her until she faltered and glanced away. I guessed she might be ashamed, except I didn't know what that looked like on her.

The silence dragged out.

"I considered an abortion. I couldn't go through with it," she said. As much as both women repulsed me, I'd never wished that Elaine hadn't been born. "I shouldn't have told Bobby I was pregnant. I wanted to have the baby adopted. He wouldn't agree to it. He promised to raise the boy and keep his mouth shut. I knew he wasn't trustworthy."

What the…? It was Caroline? I'd guessed wrong that Elaine was Tony's mother.

I did some quick math. Caroline was eighteen when she had Elaine, who was now twenty-eight. Tony was six years old, making Caroline forty when he was born and Bobby twenty-nine.

"I'd only guessed you were somehow connected to Tony," I said. "Bobby didn't tell me you're his mother.

You just did."

Her skin took on a green hue as if she might be sick.

"And like I said, I don't give a shit about your past," I repeated with a sigh. "What is it you want from me today?"

She straightened her shoulders once more. "I'm asking you to put in a good word for Elaine with the prosecuting attorney. Please, Madisen. If you request leniency, he might reduce her sentence. He would listen to you."

Really? After all I'd suffered at their hands, she was asking me to help reduce Elaine's punishment? I clenched my jaw to repress a scornful laugh. Not in a million years.

I watched a squirrel across the street stealing seeds from a birdfeeder. One of Tabs's sayings came to mind: Don't look a gift horse in the mouth.

"Okay, Caroline. Tell you what I'll do. It's time you admitted you're no better than any other human being on the planet. Stop beating others down to elevate yourself. If you put an end to your vicious gossip—and I'm saying all of it, not just about me—I promise not to report Elaine for the vandalism, and I'll keep your secrets. However, the minute I hear you've spread rumors, even something that's true, I'll add vandalism to the long list of Elaine's crimes. And I'll make sure every single person in the state finds out about your illegitimate children."

She stared, speechless for the first time.

"Do we have an agreement?"

"Yes," she muttered.

"Ask Bobby to see the prosecutor about Elaine's

sentence. It would mean more coming from him."

She winced as I drilled her with a scowl before sprinting away.

Zac was cooking breakfast when I came through the front door. He said it would be on the table by the time I finished my shower, but to be quick. He was hungry.

"Did something happen?" he asked, looking me over when I plopped onto the dining chair after cleaning up.

"You're never going to believe this—" *Wait. Can you tell him?* He was a practicing attorney.

"What?" Zac put two full plates on the table and sat down.

"Uh, if you're told who committed a crime, do you have to report it? As an officer of the court?"

"What crime?" Ignoring his food, he gave me his full attention.

"I can't tell you if you have to report it."

"It depends. Is it related to your father's shooting?"

"No. It occurred a while ago. Someone told me who did it. Well, she started to say it then stopped. When I figured it out, she nodded."

"So, you weren't told?"

"Not in words, no."

"Then I don't have to report it. What's going on?" He started eating.

"Okay. Obviously, I don't want you to tell." I relayed my conversation with Caroline. He was also astonished at her request.

"I'm glad you didn't agree to do it," he said, pride in his voice. "And even happier you've put an end to her malicious gossip."

"Do you think she'll keep her part of the bargain?"

"Yeah, I do. She has a high opinion of herself and won't want to risk ruining it. Smart idea on your part."

"By the way, what's the latest with Elaine?" I asked.

"Mrs. Van Horne posted her bail Friday afternoon. Web's opinion, and I agree, is Elaine's attorney will negotiate a plea deal rather than go to trial. Bobby recognized her car and saw Elaine driving. Convincing a jury she's innocent would be impossible."

It was good news. I didn't want to testify.

He kissed me leisurely, and every thought was driven out by the slow burn of his mouth pressed to mine.

"I have another smart idea," I said, disoriented by his kiss.

"What?"

"Make love to me."

Quick as lightning, he picked me up and carried me to the bedroom.

****

"Postcoital bliss." It had been a cliché until I'd experienced it. More like postcoital ecstasy-exhaustion. I was afraid a lifetime of it wouldn't be enough.

You'd better enjoy it while you can.

Chapter Fifteen

The question kept niggling at me, try as I might to forget it. I told myself it wasn't important. That it could start a fight with Zac. It slipped out, regardless of my intentions.

"You knew Lauren was my sister?"

"Yes," Zac said, unfazed. Like he expected I'd get around to asking. He traced lines along my collarbone with his index finger, pausing to drop an occasional kiss on my neck. "She asked me if you'd be okay with it."

"And you didn't tell me," I accused. "You're the one who lectures me about how I need to communicate more." It was harsh, even to my own ears.

"It wasn't my place," he said without irritation. "It was her news to tell. She wanted to wait until you were ready."

"I don't know if I'll ever be ready," I said, my annoyance disintegrating. "Angeline is my sister."

"Lauren just wants to spend time with her siblings. Mom was honest with her. She always knew Clyde had a family and she was a secret. She felt abandoned."

"She was lucky he didn't pay attention to her."

"With hindsight, we know that's true," Zac agreed. "As a child, she didn't understand why she couldn't be with her sisters. It was painful."

"Look, I feel for a little girl who wasn't allowed to be with her family. I just don't see why I have to welcome her with open arms as an adult."

"That's pretty cold."

Frowning, I looked away. "Please don't scold me. It's hard to describe. Angeline and I were like one soul in two bodies. Intertwined. We had different personalities but still understood what the other needed. And we didn't have to say how we felt. We automatically knew. I'll never have that bond, that same kind of link, again. It's a betrayal to even try."

"Thank you for telling me that." He pressed his lips to my temple. "I get no one can replace Angeline. What if you thought of Lauren the same way as Linda Marie and Teresa? More like extended family?"

I shifted onto my side and ran my palm along the muscles of his chest. I was close to Linda Marie and Teresa; more than friends because they were Aunt Ceci's nieces, and we had grown up together. Lauren was still a stranger, though she'd put herself in harm's way to save me. Twice. Like a sister would.

"Okay. I'll try to think of her like a cousin. Spend time with her."

"Speaking of extended family, we're going to dinner at Uncle José and Aunt Marie's."

"And you invited Lauren," I said. "I didn't realize I was agreeing to start tonight."

"You'll do fine. Tabs is coming with Randy."

"Why? She doesn't usually come to family dinners."

"She's your family, too, and, by extension, part of mine," he explained. "Carlos organized it, so I told him to invite them. For the first time, my brother wants to introduce us to a girl."

"You're kidding! I thought he was a noattachments kind of guy."

"Yeah, he was. Until now."

I pondered Carlos having a girlfriend for a second, then chewed my lip. Having to face the family's disappointment in me was overwhelming.

****

"Come on, gorgeous, you've stalled long enough." Zac called me out on my delay tactic. I'd spent a huge amount of time on my hair and makeup.

"I don't want to go," I whined.

"That's why you need to. You'll feel better after you get it over with."

"You're probably right, which is why I should call you a 'sasshole.' You make me do stuff that's good for me."

The snark prompted a kiss.

We were the last ones to arrive; Zac had to park down the street. We held hands walking to the cream brick house. It was on the outskirts of Clantonville, about half a mile from the car repair shop Uncle José had owned and operated over twenty years. He had a reputation around the community as an honest mechanic who could fix anything for a reasonable price. If the car wasn't worth it, he'd tell you. Carlos had worked at the garage for ten years as a mechanic. Recently he'd begun scheduling employee shifts and ordering inventory.

We sat on the floor in the living room. Zac put his arm around me. Teresa and Josh, Linda Marie, and Randy said hello. Tabs didn't greet me but didn't glare at me either. I took it as a positive sign. Lauren introduced me to Matthew, who thanked me for finding Grace. He was attractive: fair-skinned with dark hair and nerdy black plastic glasses that reminded me of Clark Kent. Uncle José sat by Sheriff Rey on the opposite side of the room from them. They both glowered.

"Grace not tagging along?" Zac asked Lauren.

"No, she's with Matthew's mom for the evening."

I was disappointed I wouldn't get to meet her.

"Can I get you water or tea, Zac? A soda? Maddie?" Aunt Marie asked as she passed iced tea to Sheriff Rey and Lauren.

"No, thanks," Zac answered, and I shook my head.

The front door opened, and Carlos came in leading a girl by the hand. She looked about twenty-five. She was slim, five foot six, and had long brown hair with red highlights. Her eyes caught my attention. They were huge and a fascinating green-blue color. She seemed to shrink a little when we looked at her with open curiosity.

"I want you all to meet someone I care about very much," Carlos said, hugging her to his side. He kissed her head. "Her name is Pandora. I call her Andie."

Carlos's presentation was out-of-character, and I exchanged a baffled look with Linda Marie.

"She's kind of nervous to meet the family. If, for once, you could mind your manners and not mob her, I'd appreciate it."

We scoffed at Carlos's implication we lacked etiquette. He was the rowdiest one of the bunch. He introduced each of us around the room, and she greeted everyone. Teresa and Josh gave up their seats for them, teasing Carlos that it demonstrated our innate ability to be polite.

"I wanted to get a few things out in the open with

the whole family," Carlos said, nodding to me. "Now you've met Andie, why don't you go next, Maddie? Tell us what's happened the last few days."

Hand wringing had to substitute for pacing, since the room was crowded. The third telling wasn't easier. I related the story again in detail, knowing they'd be unsatisfied with less and would ask questions until they'd digested every aspect. I included what Web had told me about Lauren staking out my father's house, following me to Aunt Ceci's, and then returning to wait for me. She nodded in encouragement. At her implicit support, I shed unexpected tears.

"Even knowing how evil my father is, I didn't think he'd retaliate by taking Grace," I said to Lauren and Matthew. "I'm sorry you got dragged into it. You almost got shot. And Aunt Ceci's house…I'll miss it, and I know you all will too."

"We're just glad you're okay," Teresa said, leaning over to hug me.

"It's not your fault," Lauren admonished. "You couldn't have known what he would do. Besides, you saved my life that night."

"Thank you. I hope that, as family, you can understand why I challenged my father. I was driven by the need to be free of my past." I lowered my head and swiped my cheek.

"Of course, we understand," Aunt Marie said. I glanced around. The men had sympathetic or confused expressions, while the women looked compassionate and nodded in agreement. Except for Tabs. She stared at her lap.

"Do you understand, Tabs?" I asked.

She raised her head and sniffled. "Yes, I do. But

next time you're in a fever to get yourself killed, you'd better take me with you. I'll have your back, like Tonto to your Lone Ranger."

"You know, in Spanish *tonto* means 'stupid,' right?" Uncle José muttered.

"Then Maddie will be Tonto. Suits her better," Tabs said with a snort.

I got up and wrapped her in a hug. She pretended to pout, and everyone laughed except Carlos. He was fiddling with his phone.

Suddenly tired, I was content to sit by Zac and let the swirl of conversation pass over me. Carlos went to the front door, though no one had knocked.

He returned with his arm around his mother.

Deborah was in her late fifties, slim and pretty, a natural beauty who drew admiration regardless of her age. I'd seen her only once, from a short distance at the cemetery. Lauren shared her clear complexion and full mouth.

The hum of voices fell off, and the room grew uncomfortable. Zac gasped. Sheriff Rey jerked forward, jaw clenched, and hands fisted. Uncle José frowned. The set of Deborah's chin indicated her resolve to face the people who'd disowned her thirty years ago. She mangled a tissue with trembling fingers.

"I'm sure you're all aware," Carlos said, "how angry I was when Mom showed up out of the blue, wanting to be a part of our lives. Andie convinced me to let Mom explain. When she told me what happened, I thought everyone else should hear it too."

"I don't have to listen to this," Sheriff Rey said, standing.

"Dad, please?" Carlos said. "I know I put you

through hell growing up. Since I got my head on straight, I've tried not to be a burden. This is the one time, as an adult, I'm asking more of you. Can you put your pain aside and listen to her story?"

Sheriff Rey stared at Carlos like he wanted to punch him. At last, he relented and sat with crossed arms.

Carlos led Deborah to his chair and stood behind her, resting a hand on her shoulder. She gazed at a spot on the wall when she wasn't looking at her lap. She spoke in a small voice, and I strained to catch her words.

"It's been thirty-two years since Rey got the job of county deputy. He was so excited. It was what he'd always wanted. He worked hard to build a good reputation, putting in a lot of hours. Sometimes fifty, even sixty a week. It seemed his work was more important than everything else. More than our marriage and the boys. And I was lowest on the priority list. We started dating at sixteen, and, for the first time, I wondered if he and I were going to be okay.

"The day of my twenty-fifth birthday, Rey had to work. He promised me he would leave on time for once and take me out to celebrate. With a ten-month-old and a four-year-old, and Rey working those hours, our time together was scarce. I tried to be understanding. It was hard, and I missed him terribly. I spent my evenings getting the boys to sleep, cleaning or doing laundry, then going to bed alone."

Deborah's voice grew steadier as she spoke. "Anyway, I'd sent the boys over to Cecilia's early and got ready. It'd been a while since I'd made the extra effort to put up my hair, do my makeup, and wear a

The Art of Being Broken

nice dress. To feel pretty. When five fifteen came and Rey was due home, my stomach fluttered. Then it was five thirty, then five forty-five. Around six o'clock, he phoned to say an emergency call had just come in, and it was bad. An accident involving a semi-truck. Everyone in the department was needed. That was all. No 'happy birthday, dear.' No 'so sorry, we'll have to reschedule.' He hung up."

Her eyes misted. "I was so hurt, I cried. Then I realized what he'd said. The call came in right before six. If he'd left at five o'clock like he'd promised, he wouldn't have heard about the accident. And that made me more furious than I could remember. I thought, 'Fine, Rey. You stay and do your job. I'm going out for my birthday.'

"I went to Frank's Bar and Grill." She closed her eyes a moment, then continued. "The place on the courthouse square. I ordered an appetizer of potato skins and a margarita. It tasted strong, and I could hardly drink it at first. I hadn't had alcohol for two years. I sipped it as I ate, watching people come and go, feeling lonely and sorry for myself."

She glanced at me, her eyes a silent plea. "Your father came in, looking sophisticated and handsome in his expensive suit and silk tie. I hadn't spoken to Clyde before. I only knew he was a defense lawyer with a reputation for never losing a case. He sat beside me and complimented my dress and hair, saying I looked stunning. That's the word he used. 'Stunning.' By then, my drink was gone. He insisted on buying me another when he found out it was my birthday.

"He was charming, telling stories and making me laugh. I was starved for attention, and he lavished it on me. Made me feel special. At ten o'clock, I decided it was time to get home. I went to the ladies' room, then stopped to say goodnight to Clyde and thank him for the company. He wanted me to stay longer. To appease him, I sat and finished what was left of my drink. He insisted on walking me to my car.

"Next thing I knew, I woke up in the passenger seat with an awful headache. I was nauseated and confused. 'What in the world happened?' I thought. I'd had a buzz but didn't realize I'd drunk enough to pass out. It was after two in the morning. Rey was going to be upset I'd been out so late."

Deborah daubed her eyes and sipped from the glass Lauren handed her. "I drove straight home. Rey wasn't there. I went to bed, still angry he'd missed my birthday, and never told him I'd gone out for drinks.

"The next day, I felt sore, as if I'd had rough sex. Not yet understanding what had happened, I persuaded myself it was hormonal. I wasn't one hundred percent regular after having Zac. I brushed it off as some sort of postpartum condition." Her voice broke. We waited until she gathered herself. "I missed my period the next two months. I was horrified when a home pregnancy test was positive. Rey and I were having a difficult phase and hadn't been intimate. Still, I loved him more than life itself."

Lauren placed a hand over Deborah's, who took a shaky breath. "For the first time, Rey came home that day for lunch. He found me hysterical and pushed me to explain. I tried to tell him what had happened. After he saw the pregnancy test, he refused to listen. He accused me of cheating, which explained why we hadn't made love for so long. Then he got a suitcase, shoveled my clothes into it and took the car key off the ring. He threw them on the porch, shoved me out the door, and locked it.

"I stayed with my sister and her husband in Lee's Summit until I delivered Lauren. It was difficult to crawl out of bed each morning. I blamed myself for getting so drunk I passed out and was taken advantage of. I was paralyzed by remorse and depressed over losing Rey."

A glance at Sheriff Rey revealed his scowl had changed to an expression of shock.

"My sister convinced me to go to a women's support group," she went on. "It helped me get back on my feet. Two of the girls I became friends with were suspicious about me blacking out. They urged me to ask around. When Lauren was nine months old, I talked to the bartender at Frank's. I asked him if he'd seen anything unusual that night. He denied it, but he was nervous. I told him I didn't think he was being straight with me and asked for the truth. He finally said he'd never admit Clyde Chandler had slipped a roofie into a woman's drink. That no one could cross Chandler and get away with it."

Deborah blew out a long sigh. "So, without him to verify my claim, I decided not to report it. At least knowing Clyde had drugged me lifted a little of my shame."

"That bastard!" Sheriff Rey growled, fists clenched once more. "He used you to get to me. I'd given testimony at a trial that convinced a jury to convict his client. Clyde hated me for spoiling his perfect record." He walked to Deborah and dropped to his knees. "My God, baby. I'm so sorry. Can you ever forgive me? The thought you'd been with another man crushed me. I had to get you out before you told me who he was. I didn't trust myself not to kill him. All the wasted years. My life has been empty without you." He laid his head in her lap. She brushed tentative fingers through his hair, fat tears rolling to her chin.

"We should give Mom and Dad some space," Carlos said. Looking shell-shocked, we filtered out the sliding doors into the backyard.

Lauren put her arm around my shoulders as we walked. I didn't shrug her off.

"You knew what Father did?" I asked.

"Yes. Mom told me before Aunt Ceci's funeral."

"I'm sorry."

"Maddie, it's not your fault. Don't apologize for him."

"Oh, I've been thoughtless," I said. "I should have helped you. With the arrangements. You had to handle Father's funeral and burial by yourself."

Lauren's mouth hung open and her brows shot up. "What do you mean? Father didn't die."

Chapter Sixteen

I lost time. Minutes that I couldn't account for. I sat on Zac's lap in a patio chair, resting against his chest.

He whispered, "You're okay. Take a deep breath. That's it."

"He was gone," I murmured. "I saw him. He was dead."

"It's all right. Keep breathing."

Reality had no place for Father. If he was alive, the universe no longer made sense. Would autumn come after winter, or the moon fall from the sky?

"How—What will I do?" I asked.

"You'll get through it. I'll be right beside you." Zac pushed my hair behind my ear.

"Are you okay?" Lauren asked.

"I don't know. How did he survive?"

"After you left, I did what you said and called 911. The EMTs got to work on him right away," she explained, pulling a chair over. "The life flight helicopter landed in front of the house about fifteen minutes later. They took him to University Medical Health Center. It has the largest neurosurgery department.

"I told the officers what had happened. Even though I was frantic to find Grace, you were smart to make me stay. The deputies were suspicious. They would've arrested me if I'd left.

"I've been talking to a Dr. Blundell at the hospital. The bullet went in above Father's ear, exiting at the base of his skull on the right side. He's in a coma. Sometimes he responds to commands to open his eyes and squeeze the doctor's hand. He's on medication to prevent brain swelling. At this point, there's nothing to do but wait."

I fastened Lauren with a vacant stare. It made her uncomfortable. She added, "The doctor said trying to predict if or when he'll recover is useless. Just to be prepared for any outcome and the choices that go with it."

"No! I mean—I can't make those kinds of decisions. You know Father and I don't exactly have a loving relationship."

"I don't think I can make them either," Lauren said. "What about your mother? Could she take over his care?"

I shook my head. "Father had her declared legally incompetent."

I remembered what Angeline had said I should tell Lauren. I stood carefully and motioned for her to follow me. I whispered, "Please, could you keep handling his care? I just can't, and I trust your judgment. I know it's a burden on top of your difficulties getting pregnant. You can stop worrying. It's going to be okay."

Lauren's eyes almost jumped out of her head. Without a word, she gave a small nod.

****

Fury churned in me. "Why wasn't I told he was alive?" I yelled, pacing like a caged animal. "I can't believe you kept this from me!" Once we were at Zac's, the path of least resistance had led me to anger. The dim awareness I was being irrational was no match for my rage. It was my last, desperate effort to keep from falling apart.

Unaffected by my accusations, Zac waited for my emotional firestorm to burn itself out. After twenty minutes, my seams burst. Hoarse sobs replaced my shouts, and my knees failed. Zac scooped me into his arms as I collapsed and carried me to bed. He held me close during the hours I whispered one phrase to myself until exhaustion stripped it from me. I fell asleep with the letters burned into my heart: I H A T E H I M.

...Arms around each other, we sit on the floor in my old room. I look at the empty glass I'd left on the desk. The water hadn't washed away the bitter tang of hatred.

Angeline releases me, and I reluctantly drop my arm.

"You have to see him before you leave. You know that," she says.

I refuse to accept it. I wasn't ready to see Father. *"You wanted me to tell Lauren not to worry about having a baby. She was too surprised to ask how I found out. When she does, I'll have to lie."*

"Why can't you tell her the truth?"

"Because she'll think I'm crazy."

"Nah, she wouldn't."

I wish everyone were as open-minded. I'm happy Angeline believes in goodness. That she hung on to what little innocence she had left at the end...

****

Monday, September 28
The first day of the week was one I'd never been

partial to. This Monday might prove to be the worst. I woke with puffy eyes and felt horrible about the way I'd acted. Zac sat on the bed like a kind-hearted saint, a steaming mug in his hand.

"Morning," he said.

"Hello, handsome." I pushed myself up and took a sip, relieved he was speaking to me after the way I'd treated him.

"Thank you. Oh, you meant the coffee." He pretended to sulk.

"Yes, I did. Because you're beyond handsome. You treat me better than I deserve."

His smile at my compliment was adorable. "You do deserve it. How are you feeling?"

"I'm a mess." I kissed his cheek. "Thanks for being patient with me yesterday. I'm so sorry I blamed you."

"You get a pass on this one. You've been hit by too many emotional bombs lately. I knew I wasn't the one you were upset with. You want to talk about it?"

"I know I should let it out. I just don't know where to start."

"Last night, you kept repeating, 'I hate him,' " he said, making me cringe. "Oh, I don't blame you. I hate him, too." He sat with me and guided my head to his shoulder. "Start with that."

I was too tired to fight it.

"I hate him. There. I said it. I hate my father for what he did to Angeline. I hate him for being cold and distant, for not caring." With that, the cork holding my frustrations popped. I jumped from one hurt to the next on my laundry list of pain. "I never remember him asking how I was or how my day went. And everything was my fault. If Father had a bad day in court? He couldn't prepare the night before because of my noise. Once, he blamed me because the shaker on the table ran out of salt. I was six.

"He never cared about anyone but himself. He was a bully. A bulldozer. From what your mom said, he had a reputation in town of making people pay if—" I cut myself off, shaking my head. "Why don't you despise me?" I asked.

When Zac responded with a blank look to my question, I said, "Yesterday, you learned Father was the reason you grew up without your mother. I've been caught up in my own issues and forgot to ask if you're doing okay."

"I don't despise you," he answered, raking a hand through his hair. "I am pissed at your father. When Mom told us what had happened, I finally understood what it means to want to kill a man. Before, when your father hurt you, I was angry but convinced myself to let it go, to concentrate on supporting you, knowing together we'd get through it.

"When I heard he was the reason my family was torn apart? All the suffering he caused? I can't take it away or make it right. I feel helpless. I admit I didn't appreciate what you were going through. I'm starting to grasp what you meant about feeling like a victim and needing to be in control." His voice was vehement, but he looked unruffled.

"How can you be so calm? I was a screaming monster, taking my anger out on you."

"I have my moments. Usually, I can keep it under wraps until I get to the dojo. If Master Chen's class isn't enough to get it out of my system, I beat on the sandbag. It's the same thing you do when you run."

"I zone out and de-stress or work through stuff that bugs me during a run. When I'm overwhelmed, I turn into an evil bitch and yell at my boyfriend for no reason."

"I'm man enough to handle your bitchiness, woman!" he teased, pounding a fist on his chest.

I groaned and hid my face.

"Today, I'll run with you. We can picture your father's face on every bug we stomp."

I rolled my eyes, and he kissed my forehead. We crawled out of bed and changed into our running gear.

On the street, Zac let me set the pace. After we'd gone about a mile, he got in front and I followed him, paying no attention to the route. Our surroundings became a blur as I thought of my father and zeroed in on my hatred of him. I tried to recall every negative feeling, then pictured it flowing down my arms and out through my hands before I went on to the next. One bad recollection after another was discarded like toxic waste.

"Maddie!" Zac said, gasping. He stopped and put his hands on his knees, panting hard. "You trying to run all the way to Kansas?"

"No," I said, panting too. I saw we were in his neighborhood. "How far did we go?"

"About ten miles. You're a machine."

"I worked through some of the baggage. It was good." Zac nodded and took my hand as we walked to his house.

****

We'd had an unhurried shower and breakfast after our run. Then we'd made love. Zac's tenderness left me wanting. I'd needed unrestrained passion—an exuberant, life-affirming connection that could purge the remaining enmity that clung to my skin. The tumultuous sex made Zac complain I'd used every ounce of stamina he had. He dragged himself to the office for his afternoon appointments. I was tired, too, and content.

I ate lunch and wasn't sure what to do with myself next. I didn't want to take a nap and couldn't visit with Tabs because she was at work. Earlier, she'd sent me a text to see if I was doing okay and invited us to their place for dinner. I answered that we'd be there at six thirty, and I was fine. She was a good friend. I thanked her and sent my apologies for not seeing each other as much as we'd planned. I was leaving for Texas the day after tomorrow.

That meant I had to make a decision.

Our days together had brought Zac and me closer, and I'd made progress in my effort to open my heart. I flipped on the TV, wondering if I should tell him about Angeline. Part of me wanted to keep her a secret. Our time together was sacrosanct. I couldn't bear it if Zac doubted her existence. And, maybe it was silly, but I was nervous Angeline might disappear if I told someone. On the other hand, I worried about keeping things from Zac. The omission felt like a lie.

There was a knock at the door. I checked the peephole. Detective Hanson was waiting on the step.

Wondering why he was here, I opened the door halfway.

He returned my stare without expression, except for a slight drawing of his brows. He gave me a nod and looked at the ground. "May I come in?"

I didn't want to talk to him. However, he looked

devastated, his shoulders bowed with an invisible load. I moved aside and motioned to the sofa.

"I brought your purses from your father's house. For now, we'll keep your gun as evidence." I didn't move to take the bags. He placed them on the coffee table as he sat and gazed at his hands. I sat, too, and waited.

Finally, in a low voice, he said, "I came to apologize. I was out of line when I accused you of setting the fire and collaborating with your father to kidnap Grace. I'm sorry." He ran a hand down his chin. "I can't live with it anymore."

That didn't make sense. His regret for being an asshole was nice, but wasn't provoking a suspect during questioning part of the job?

"Can't live with what?" I asked.

"You see, about fifteen years ago, a rookie detective had a lapse of judgment. He made one mistake that would have ended a career, a good reputation, and a marriage. Ruined the rest of his life."

He changed the direction of the conversation, saying, "I don't believe you were with Cecilia Ortiz when she passed. Have you watched a loved one die from cancer, Ms. Chandler?"

I shook my head.

"I'd never wish it on my worst enemy. It's a cruel disease. When nothing more could be done for my mother, she asked to come home. She didn't have insurance, and hospice was out of the question. The pain medication cost a fortune. I had three kids under eight. My sister Amelia had moved in with us the year before, along with her little boys. Amelia worked hard. Even with two jobs, her minimum wage didn't stretch far enough. Then, my wife had to quit her job to take care of Mom. Every day, seeing the pain she was in? I couldn't stand it.

"Illegally acquired painkillers were locked in the evidence room. One day they disappeared. The wrong person found out who took them. All these years, he held on to the proof to use when he needed someone to do his dirty work."

Lauren's description of the man throwing the Molotov cocktail came to me. A big person…three hundred fifty pounds. And Angeline had mentioned Father's blackmail.

"The fire?" I whispered.

For a fraction of a second, I saw it in Hanson's eyes. The icy sheen of self-recrimination. He covered it instantly. I understood he didn't want pity and would never expect it.

"My youngest boy is almost seventeen. Though he might not admit it, I think he admires the detective work his dad does. How I gather evidence to put away the bad guys, so they don't hurt more people. He's expressed interest in going to college to study criminology."

Trying to make sense of his story, I offered no response.

Hanson cleared his throat. "Well, my official visit today is to share the fire chief's report. It said something strange happened. The fire had one origination point, from the incendiary device thrown into the kitchen. That's odd because he found a second bottle in the living room. Accelerant should have spilled from it, causing another point of ignition or, at the least, a scorch mark. The rag stuffed inside went out. Then zilch. Nothing happened." He glanced at me, then away. "Maybe the liquid was a slower burning fuel. Maybe it was just dumb luck. Or it could be the bottle was empty. Fortunate for you, though. The front door wasn't blocked, giving you a chance to escape."

Hanson said no more. I was slow to comprehend his intent. He was putting the decision in my hands by confessing. If I reported him, I was sure he'd tell his superiors the truth. But why? The consequences for his crimes would be severe as a member of law enforcement. And he could have gotten away with both offenses. Chances were slim my father would expose him. Even if he came out of the coma, he ran the risk of implicating himself.

I realized Hanson had defied my father by leaving the second bottle empty. Hanson also said he couldn't live with what he'd done and came to me.

"Were there any other lapses of judgment in this detective's career?" I asked.

He looked at me with a steady eye. "No. Nothing. Living with that guilt was more than enough."

I weighed the information. Did I want him punished for destroying Aunt Ceci's house? Part of me did. Yet ripping apart Hanson's family and ruining his career wouldn't undo the damage. And I was done. I didn't want to see more people suffer because of Father.

"I think," I said slowly, "when the fire started, it was more than luck that got me out alive. Who knows? I could have a guardian angel watching over me." I looked at the detective. "It was dark that night, and no one saw him clearly. Angel or not, he can't be identified."

Hanson let out an enormous breath and smiled over

his double chin. "You're an honorable person, Ms. Chandler. Thank you." He patted my shoulder. "You've been through a lot. I hope you can put it all behind you. If you ever need help of any kind, I'll be there." He strode to the door with a lighter step. As he went out, he added, "Make sure your boyfriend treats you like a queen. You deserve to be happy."

Chapter Seventeen

Zac sang, "Honey, I'm home!" It woke me from my doze.

"I'm in here," I answered. In the half minute it took him to walk to the bedroom, I remembered talking with Angeline as I'd napped.

"...He's practically a vegetable. He won't know I'm there," I say.

"You can't be sure. I bet he can hear you."

"What would I tell him?" I argue. " 'I hope you get well soon so you can rot in prison'? It wouldn't do any good."

"Sure, it would. Tell him whatever you need to. You'll feel better."

I look away and shake my head.

"Please? It'll help," she says.

The thought of being in the same room with Father makes me want to throw up, even if Angeline is right. When I look at her, her chin is quivering. I can't stand to make her cry.

"Okay, I'll visit him," I say, not promising to talk.

She understands, nodding...

"Sleeping, huh?" Zac said, seeing me in bed.

"I was tired after all our exercise this morning," I answered, sitting up. "And I had a visitor. Detective Hanson."

"Why did he come by?" Zac asked.

I told Zac, trusting him with the information.

"Wow. Are you going to report him?"

"No. Hanson's been through enough. I believe him about Father's blackmail, and that he didn't put fuel in the second Molotov cocktail. I know what it's like to be judged in the court of public opinion. I don't want his wife and children to go through that."

"You're more forgiving than I might've been. Well, it's one less thing for you to worry about. You have enough on your plate."

****

Zac stopped the truck in front of Aunt Ceci's house. It didn't look too bad. Soot above the broken windows was the only obvious sign of the fire. A tiny ray of hope flickered inside. I knew moderate smoke damage could be cleaned.

But the intact front was misleading. From the back, I saw it couldn't be saved. A quarter of the building was all that stood. The rest was gutted by the blaze. The smell of smoke floated over piles of snowy ash and black debris scattered with two-by-fours.

"I'm sorry, Aunt Ceci," I said. Thankful Zac was there to support me, I leaned on him.

"She knows it's not your fault. If you're safe, she wouldn't care about the house."

"I just..." I couldn't say more.

"I know you wanted her house to remember her by. It meant a lot to both of us." He pressed his cheek to my hair as I sniffled. "But memories are held in our heart, not in a building."

I nodded, knowing he was right. It still hurt.

"Let's get to Tabs and Randy's," he said, taking my hand. "She'll send out the National Guard if we're late."

I smiled at him, his face blurred by my tears, and let him lead me forward.

****

Tabs opened the door when we pulled up, and I ran to her. As always, her hug gave me strength.

"Will it have to be torn down?" she asked. I could only nod, and she embraced me again. "Here, I poured you a glass of wine. It's the Pinot Grigio you like."

I settled on the sofa. Tabs knew I wasn't up to talking and was content with my occasional sounds of interest. She passed on greetings from her parents, who'd moved back to Alabama, and kept the conversation light. After a yummy dinner of pot roast with carrots and potatoes, and a dessert of bread pudding, we played cards. An evening of laughter was the perfect antidote to my melancholy. I cherished those moments with my best friend.

****

Tuesday, September 29

By nine o'clock in the morning, we stood outside Father's hospital room at the University Medical Health Center.

Zac wore a tie and dress shirt and carried his briefcase. Although he would've gone in with me, he accepted my decision to see Father alone. He glanced back as he walked to the elevator as if to be sure I wouldn't change my mind. When it dinged, he entered without hesitation and went to his appointment.

I remained in the hall, staring at the door as if a rattlesnake might lurk behind it. When I finally peered in, the figure on the bed was too small. I checked the number again. Three thirty-two. It was the right room. I slipped inside, pressing myself against the wall.

Nothing happened. I'd half expected Father to leap up and grab me.

He'd conditioned me well. *No more fear.* I was determined to be strong. On the far wall, a display of numbers by his bed changed every few seconds: ninety-two, sixty-nine, one twenty-six. The digits revealed his oxygen level, heart rate, and blood pressure. Proving he lived.

One step. I picked up a heavy foot and moved it forward. One more. Awkwardly, I shambled to an upholstered chair, sank into it, and forced myself to appear relaxed.

The window was covered with a partially drawn shade. The room was neither too bright nor too dark. Not too hot or cold. Not black or white. No right or wrong. Judgment was absent in this place of healing.

A slight mound under the blankets, Father was no longer imposing. The demon of my childhood had been reduced to an ordinary man. I stood and moved closer. His head was bandaged; otherwise, his features were familiar. He breathed peacefully, almost unmoving. For the first time, he was the helpless one. At my mercy. I could've covered his nose and mouth with one hand until zeros flashed across the monitor, and he'd be out of my life forever.

Not trusting myself, I clasped my hands behind me and sat in the chair. He remained oblivious.

At length, I whispered, "Angeline wanted me to come. To talk to you while I had the chance. Speak my piece." I stopped, suddenly furious. I gritted my teeth but was unable to hold in the pain. "Why were you so cruel? I only wanted my father to love me. I don't understand why you couldn't. A parent is supposed to watch over his children. Instead, you became the evil we feared." I bounded from the chair to stand over him.

"And Angeline," I seethed. "I should have protected her. Instead, she shielded me. I didn't see the hell you were putting her through." My voice oozed with such malice I hardly recognized it.

"She says she's forgiven you, and she wants me to, as well." I brought up clenched fists. "I'll never forgive you. Every day I have on earth, I'll hate you for hurting Angeline. You called her 'my Angel.' But she was never yours. I'm the one she loves! She's mine."

Father's lids crept open. From one unfocused eye, a tear leaked out, slid down, and disappeared into his hair.

I left Father, promising myself I'd never see him again. I rode the elevator to the ground floor. Zac sat by the main entrance, briefcase at his feet.

"How did it go?" he asked, standing.

"All right," I said, not wanting to talk about it yet. "How's Bobby doing?"

"He said he's feeling better and can't wait to get out of here and home to Tony." Zac raised his brows. "And he asked if you and I were together."

Oops. "Yeah, about that. The day I saw him I was upset. I told him you broke up with me. What did you say?"

"I said we're definitely together and asked why he wanted to know. He said if I was stupid enough to give up a once-in-a-lifetime girl like you, he didn't want me as his lawyer. And he'd ask you out. I informed Bobby I'm never letting you go." Zac kissed my hair and put a hand on my back. "Let's get some lunch."

****

Zac said, "We need to have a talk."

We'd just gotten home after visiting the hospital, and I wanted some alone time to process seeing Father. However, Zac's tone signaled our conversation was important to him.

In a split second, I made up my mind. With a shuddering breath, I nodded. It was now or never. I was scheduled to leave tomorrow.

"Yes, I've got something to tell you, too."

Surprise and concern sailed across his face.

"Let's go outside," I said. "I need some air."

"You want to go to the park?"

"Okay," I said, rushing out the door.

During the ten-minute drive, uncertainties rippled over me, and I wiped sweaty palms on my legs. This is it. How will he take it? I wanted time. More time with him, just as we were. Telling him my secret would change the way he saw me, change things between us. It might even end us.

When we arrived, I stumbled out of the truck before it stopped and headed toward the lake. Cool air was blowing from the water. I wanted to stuff it by the handful into my lungs. Zac spread an old blanket on the grass and sat. I was too twitchy to join him.

"You're not going to leave me, are you?" he asked.

"Of course not," I said with a huff. "I'm just nervous about what I need to say."

"Baby, don't worry. Even if you said you were dying or planned to donate your brain to science or were from a galaxy far, far away, I'd stick by you."

"You're being absurd."

"No, you are. I'm trying to convince you whatever

you say, we'll be fine."

"I'm insane," I blurted. "I mean, I'm showing signs of mental instability." Words burbled out as I paced in front of him. "Because I talk to Angeline. We're together in my dreams, and we discuss what's going on in my life. She helped me recover memories of our childhood. She told me where to find the photos incriminating my father and why Elaine and Caroline van Horne have always hated me." I chanced a peek at Zac.

His incredulous expression said it all.

"You don't believe she's real."

"I'm surprised is all." His face became neutral as he studied me.

I turned my back on his skepticism.

"Maddie? Please sit with me."

Biting my lip, I shuffled to him and slumped to the ground. "I can guess what you're thinking," I said when I could speak. "You assume talking to Angeline in dreams is just my imagination. That's not it. She protects me. She sees and tells me things I couldn't know otherwise.

"It started a few weeks after her funeral, when she told me where to find my missing necklace. I know it sounds odd, but she kept me from losing my mind after she died. I was miserable. Without her to talk to, I would've given up." I propped my head on my fist. "I heard her again when I came back this summer. On the way to Aunt Ceci's wake from the airport."

Zac gaped at me. I looked away. Seeing his doubt would unknit me.

"What do you mean, 'heard her again'?"

"After I left town, she didn't talk to me. The whole

ten years I was away, I never saw her."

"So, it's only when you're in Clantonville?" he asked, and I nodded. "I guess that makes sense."

"How does any of this make sense?"

"I don't think you're unstable if the only sign of it doesn't surface for ten years." He mulled it over. "What if she's tethered to the area and can't go far? Or she speaks to you when she sees you're in trouble, and it's a coincidence you're here."

"So, you believe me?"

"Honestly? I don't know if I believe in ghosts." He lifted my fingers to his lips. It calmed me somewhat. "I've heard of stranger things. If you believe it, I respect that. I'm glad you're comforted and have her help."

"Then, you don't believe me." I focused on my hand in his.

"Does it matter? The way I feel about you hasn't changed."

"It matters if you think I'm mentally unbalanced. What if she drives me to do something irrational, like Mother?"

"Oh, that's why you're worried about ending up like her." He shook his head. "Your mother's mental illness was likely what led her to murder Angeline. And guilt for that, on top of her instability, drove her to attempt suicide. Baby, some things you do may be crazy, but I have no doubt you're completely sane." He placed a gentle palm around my chin and turned my head, searching my face before touching his mouth to mine.

The sincerity of his words, bolstered by the gentle warmth of his kiss, removed my misgivings. I opened to him.

Our tongues swirled, and I understood what a gift he was. He'd accepted me without judgment. My worry lifted, and my chest flooded with joy. Helpless to stop a new surge of tears, I hiccupped.

"What is it?" he asked.

"I'm so happy you still like me."

"I feel a lot more than 'like' for you." He moved so we sat knee to knee, kissing my lids and brushing a thumb over my cheek. "We've known each other most of our lives, and you're the only woman who can see into my soul. You like who I am, without agendas or demands to change. Before we were lovers, I wasn't complete. You give me purpose.

"I'm determined to become the man you trust, the one you confide in, knowing I won't control you. The man whose voice helps you make it through the day. A good man you can be proud of. One who, by every means imaginable, convinces you that you're worthy. The man you can't live without."

"You already are."

"Madisen, what I'm trying to say is, I love you."

****

"Are you okay?" The question was like a moth wing fluttering against my skin, bringing me back to earth. I didn't know how long I'd floated in a starry ether among picture-perfect dreams.

A man sat in front of me. He had startling good looks: square jaw, sinfully tempting lips, smooth skin, black hair. And those eyes. Fascinating pools of chocolate I wanted to dive into, now looking at me with apprehension.

Unexpected, words fell from my mouth. "You

said…"

"I love you."

I blinked.

Blinked once more.

"I…" My brain was muddled. Shaking my head didn't un-muddle it. "Again."

"I love you, Maddie."

There. That singular phrase. If it were a mantra repeated a thousand times, the truth of it would remain a rare benediction. His words filled me; I was treasured.

"Zac?"

"Yes, baby?"

You can do this. "I—" I swallowed. "I la—"

Say it! Angeline yelled in my head.

"—love you, too."

"Come again?"

"I love you, Zac."

Delighted laughter burst out of him, making joy surge up my spine. He pecked my hands with quick kisses and pulled me with him as he stood. We raced hand in hand to his truck, leaving the blanket behind.

In reverse, he mashed the gas, spewing gravel from the tires. He brightened as he shifted gears. "Hey! You should ask Angeline to give you the winning lottery numbers."

"No!"

"Stock tips?"

"Zac!" I swatted at him, unable to pretend annoyance.

"Just a thought." He leaned close, laying soft lips on mine.

****

Wednesday, September 30

The dimness of early morning filled the bedroom. It was the day I had to leave. I turned carefully in Zac's arms and watched him sleep. Dawn invaded the window in slow phases. As the light grew, I studied the arc of his lips, the sweep of his jaw, and the curve of his cheek. To imprint on my mind what love looked like. The image would keep me afloat when we were apart.

His lids fluttered open, and he grazed a finger down my arm. "Good morning, beautiful," he said. "Have I told you I love you?"

"A dozen times," I answered. "Never enough."

"I do love you."

"And I love you, Zac."

I went through the motions of showering, dressing, gathering my clothes, closing my suitcase, putting my flight confirmation in my bag with my sweatshirt.

During the drive to the airport, we held hands. "I want you to consider an idea I have. Don't decide yet. Take as long as you want to think it over."

After he explained, Zac raised my knuckles to brush his lips across them, tender as a breeze.

We were quiet as the miles behind us increased along with my dread. I didn't want this. How could I let go of Zac's hand and walk away?

But I had to. To heal the open wounds of anger, pain, and frustration, I needed to go. Though Zac was willing to help me cope, I knew I had to do it on my own. By gathering every fragment of strength he believed I possessed, I had to scrape away the infected layers of my past and, with them, my fear of commitment.

****

We stood inside the airport as the last call for my

flight was announced. I got lost in Zac's expressive eyes touched with sadness.

"Don't you want a sandwich to eat on the plane?" Zac was saying. "You might get hungry later."

"No, I won't need it."

"Well, I guess it's time."

"Yes," I answered, not moving. "I love you, Zacarias Redondo. I miss you already."

"I miss you too. Remember, I'm a phone call away, whenever you need me, twenty-four seven. And I know it's a lot on top of everything else. Please, think about the idea I had."

"Yes, I will." He bent to place his lips at my ear and whispered a final promise.

I soaked in the image of his face as I passed through security, then stared at his picture on my phone until I turned it off for departure. The ache in my chest doubled as I clung to his last words. "I love you, baby. I always will."

****

"...You went to see Daddy?" Angeline asks.

"Yes. I wondered why he wasn't cuffed to the bed. If he wakes up, he might be able to escape. The nurses said, on the tiny chance that happened, he'd be too weak to get very far. Also, the bed triggers an alarm if his weight comes off." I brush her long hair away from her face. "You were right, by the way."

She blooms with satisfaction. "About what?"

"Seeing Father. It sank in. I believe it in here now," I say, tapping my chest over my heart. "He can't hurt me. I'm not scared of him anymore."

"Good. If you're not afraid of him, you'll be able to forgive him."

"I doubt it. I hate him and probably always will." I nudge her shoulder. "I never did say thank you for helping me learn the truth about what Father did. And for finding Grace. And for keeping me from giving up after you died. You always take care of me. I'd have never made it without you. I owe you everything."

"No, you don't. Besides, that's what sisters do. Take care of each other," she says. "You'll be all right now."

"Angeline?"

"You have a new sister. A whole family. Look after them, and they'll be there for you, too."

"No! It's you I need."

"You'll be fine. You're ready," she says, wrapping me in her arms.

"I love you," I finally say.

"Love you more, Maddie."

"I love you most, Angel…"

Epilogue

Thursday, November 26

The people who sang about it and celebrated it were wrong. As I stood in the fading light that gilded the fall leaves, I didn't believe in the circle of life. Our existence had a beginning and an end. In my father's case, the end came when the "plug" was pulled.

He'd deteriorated in the weeks following my return to Texas. His ability to blink or squeeze with his hands had become infrequent until, a month ago, he'd stopped reacting altogether. With no neurologic response, the doctors had advised his chance of recovery was negligible and recommended Lauren consider ending his tube feedings.

His poor prognosis and probable death gave me no misgivings. I told Lauren the decision was hers. Her struggle with the responsibility of shooting him had faded. She had no regrets about helping me that night. She'd simply refused to lose another sister.

What did bother her was Father's willingness to take her life because it benefitted him. In other words, would her decision to stop his food be influenced by a need for revenge? I didn't voice an opinion. I just listened as she talked it through. To be free of regret, I knew she had to come to her own conclusion.

"I thought withholding his food would mean he'd starve to death," she said in one of our regular phone conversations. "Evidently, people in a coma don't get hungry. He won't feel like he's starving. In his condition, he'll be gone about two weeks after the nutrition is stopped."

Eleven days after his food was withheld, the hospital notified her he'd last only a few more hours. She thanked them and explained no one would come to sit with him. He died alone.

My suitcases were packed when Lauren called to say he was gone. I packed the car with my things and started the next morning, stretching the drive from San Antonio over three days. As planned, Father's body was cremated. The ashes were waiting for me to pick up at Lawler's Funeral Home the afternoon I arrived in Clantonville. From there, I drove to the cemetery to meet Zac, Lauren, and Matthew.

The suggestion to dump his remains in the pasture behind his house was mine. Lauren preferred the more dignified option of spreading them beside Angeline. Unable to bear the thought of his angel spending eternity alone, Father had purchased adjacent plots so he and Mother could be buried beside her. Since Angeline had forgiven Father, I agreed. Lauren and I also decided we didn't want a ceremony. We would erect a simple marker inscribed only with his name and dates of birth and death.

The urn weighed less in my hands than I expected. As I carried it from the car, I could feel Father's impact on my psyche diminish. I hoped someday it would be as insubstantial as his powdery ashes. I shook some onto the ground, then passed the urn to Lauren to scatter the rest. Zac put his arm around me.

"You okay?" he asked.

"Never better. Let's get going."

We drove six miles to the Wybeck farm where a bonfire was burning in a field. Lauren and Matthew followed in their car. Tabs and Randy, and Teresa and Josh were already there. We greeted one another with hugs in the cool evening. Deborah and Sheriff Rey walked up holding hands and welcomed me like a prodigal daughter. Soon, Linda Marie, Uncle José, and Aunt Marie joined us. Carlos arrived a few minutes later. We helped ourselves to beer from the coolers and sat in camp chairs close to the fire.

To my surprise, dozens of townspeople came. Bobby Wittford walked over with a slight limp. Zac eyed him as he gave me a long hug.

"Great to see you, Madisen. You doing all right?"

"I'm wonderful. And you look fantastic! How's your leg?"

"Getting better all the time. I'll be back to work before long." He offered Zac a hand, saying, "Thanks for your help. I owe you."

"Nah, we're even now. You need a beer?" Before I had a chance to ask what they were talking about, they were out of earshot. Mrs. Wells pushed through the group gathered near me and plopped into a chair.

"Hello there, Madisen!" she said loudly. Everyone pressed closer to listen. "I heard you was going to be here tonight and thought, land sakes! There's a young woman I know 'most everybody would be glad to welcome home. I read that story in yesterday's paper. My Lord, to think life was so awful for you girls, and it happened right under our noses. We didn't suspect a thing! I'm sorry nothing was done at the time for you and your sister. I'm sure there's not a soul around who wouldn't have helped if we'd known." Heads nodded in agreement.

During my time in Texas, in three sessions a week, Mary Anne had taught me vital coping skills, knowing it might take years to come to terms with my parents' abuse and my anger at them. I'd made progress by working hard and "graduated" from my self-care program. One of my assigned tasks was writing a letter to Mother notifying her of Father's attempts on my life, his death, and my feelings about both. Another was to take Jayce Phelps's advice. I worked with him on a piece for the *Clantonville News* telling my side of the story. I'd arranged for my short biography to be published alongside my father's obituary. Though I'd prepared for a negative reaction, I hoped the townspeople wouldn't openly criticize me or accuse me of lying.

"Awful for you," Charlotte Gutshall said.

"You poor girl!" John Hanson added.

"We're here for you," Jennifer said as she hugged me.

My breath caught at their sentiments. "Thank you. Your support...Well, it means more to me than you all can underst—" Stopping to flap my hand in front of my face, I cleared my throat. When I could go on, I said, "I want to put the past behind me. I'm looking forward to the future."

"And you're here to stay?" Katie asked.

"Yes. It's time I came home to start the next chapter of my life. Zac got the idea in September during our drive to the airport. He invited me to move in with him." Katie squealed and clapped her hands amid approving mutters from the crowd.

"Well, I aim to leave you young people to your partying." Mrs. Wells heaved herself up, and Josh helped her to her car.

Conversation buzzed for the next two hours about the events that had occurred over the last four months: the vandalism of my aunt's house, an attempted vehicular manslaughter, a fire, two shootings, and a story exposing past abuse. A steady stream of people came to express empathy and welcome me home.

A voice yelled, "Everybody, if I could have your attention." Heads swiveled to Randy. "I have something y'all need to hear. I think everyone knows I been sweet on Miss Tabitha Lynn Strayer for more than five years now. Well, last night, I asked Tabitha here if she'd do me the honor of becoming my wife." A hush fell. Randy looked down, shuffling his feet. Tabs stood back a few steps, hands clasped, looking contrite. Embers crackled, sending up sparks.

"And?" someone finally asked.

"She said yes!" Randy shouted. Everyone hooted and clapped.

I sprinted to Tabs, and we jumped up and down, laughing. "Oh my God, Tabs! I'm so happy for you."

"You're not upset we announced it at your party? I thought you might cloud up and rain all over me."

"No, don't be silly!" I grabbed her fingers to see her ring. Women came over as men surrounded Randy. One buddy held up his beer, toasting one more bachelor's move to the state of matrimony.

When there was a pause in the conversation, Zac gave me a long kiss. "I have another surprise for you."

"More good news? Tell me."

"Today I went to court with Bobby. He was

officially granted custody of Tony. Caroline agreed to all the terms. She'll pay support and has visiting rights every other weekend."

"She hasn't taken an interest in him before. I wonder if she'll spend time with him."

"I think she will. Bobby told me she mentioned redecorating Elaine's bedroom for a little boy." Zac chuckled when my brows shot up. "Caroline has changed a lot since Elaine was sentenced to prison."

"That reminds me. What did Bobby mean when he said he owed you? And you answered that you were even."

"I waived my fees. He saved your life. I figured it was the least I could do."

"That was sweet. And it reminds me, I need to ask you a favor. Would having tenants move into Father's house cause problems with the estate settlement? I'd like for Josh and Teresa to live there."

"I know they still want to get out of their apartment. I'll look into it." He caught me trying to hide a yawn. "You tired? Do you want to go home?"

"Yes. I want to be alone with you," I said. With a devilish grin, he took my hand.

Lauren intercepted us. "Maddie, you two taking off?"

"Yeah, it's been a long day." I'd noticed at the cemetery Lauren glowed with the joy of an expectant mother. "By the way, congratulations!"

"Thank you! Matt and I are thrilled, and Grace is ecstatic!"

"Is it a boy or girl?"

"Too soon to know." She leaned close and whispered, "Last time you were here, you told me not to worry about conceiving. I took a pregnancy test the next day. It was negative. But three weeks later, another test showed you were right. How'd you know?"

"Well," I said, putting an arm around her, "I can't say. It's a secret."

Just then, I could've sworn I heard a giggle.

A word about the author...

As a writer, Nicole was first smitten with poetry. A piece she wrote in middle school won a state contest. Her work has been published in journals that include *The Midwest Quarterly* and *The New Press Literary Quarterly*. However, Nicole's lasting passion is writing novels about women and men who must dig deep within themselves to discover personal fortitude to face adversity.

Nicole grew up in small-town America and received a degree in Hispanic Literature. She has lived in the U.S. Southwest, West Coast, and Nevada desert. Her travels throughout Mexico, to Canada, Cuba, Israel, and Costa Rica instilled a desire to see the rest of the world. A tiny Yorkshire terrier (four pounds!) named Gigi is her sidekick.

Her web site is http://www.nicolesorrell.com.
You can follow her on Facebook
http://www.facebook.com/nicole.sorrell.author/
on Pinterest
https://www.pinterest.com/nicolesorrell73/
and Twitter
http://twitter.com/cnicolesorrell
Nicole loves to hear from readers—contact her at nicole@nicolesorrell.com.

Thank you for purchasing
this publication of The Wild Rose Press, Inc.

For questions or more information
contact us at
info@thewildrosepress.com.

The Wild Rose Press, Inc.
www.thewildrosepress.com

Milton Keynes UK
Ingram Content Group UK Ltd.
UKHW031439121024
449426UK00012B/523